DEVIL'S DUE

DEVIL'S DUE

J.P. JACKSON

Queer Space

New Orleans

Published in the United States of America and United Kingdom by

Queer Space

A Rebel Satori Imprint

www.rebelsatoripress.com

Fonts used: Section divider Castine™, title text Schooner Script™ and backcover copy Antiquarian Scribe™ are copyright © Three Islands Press (www.3ip.com)

Paperback ISBN: 978-1-60864-217-5

Ebook ISBN: 978-1-60864-218-2

Library of Congress Control Number: 2022938953

CONTENTS

PART 1

"Mr. Ronove," Elisha peeked around the heavy wooden door to my office, "If you don't leave now, you won't make your appointment."

"Hmm." Studying the paperwork in front of me, I scratched out a few words, then underlined the next sentence.

"Mr. Ronove?" Elisha appeared in front of my desk, head tilted, looking at me with obvious impatience. The unsubtle scents of amber, jasmine and cedar wood wafting off of her skin stuck in the back of my throat. Giving up on the specific wording of the contract before me, I stared at my assistant. I could tell Elisha had decided it was quitting time. Her long hair, usually pulled up and pinned with her signature bone clip, had been released. She trailed the tips of her fingernails along the wooden edge of my imported antique Gothic style bureau. Her nails were painted to perfection, which reflected how Elisha generally came to work. Sultry, but flawlessly professional. Her nails were long enough to exude a sensuousness but still able to perform her duties and

1

the blood red colour matched her spiked high heeled shoes impeccably. Her draped, woolen black skirt hugged her curvy hips, and the winter-sky grey, cowl neck blouse accentuated all the curves.

"Yes, sorry?"

"Your appointment." She tapped the diamond encrusted slim watch face on her wrist. "It's after two. You need to be there before three."

"Oh, yes. Thank you." My brows furrowed as the sparkle from a tiny white jewel pierced my gaze as she let her arm fall to her side. "That's a lovely watch. Awfully extravagant for an administrative assistant. No?"

Elisha walked over to the pronged rack standing near the door to my office. She grabbed my trench coat and briefcase, then returned to stand by my side. "The document is inside. Rodolfo is waiting for you." With the coat slung over her arm she bent over and whispered into my ear, "You forget who my boss is. He pays me very well."

"For discretion, my dear. I pay you for discretion." I turned to glare at her, one eyebrow cocked expressing my dissatisfaction. She pulled away, if only a tad. "And as much as I can appreciate the finer things, we do not want to draw attention to ourselves."

Elisha rolled her eyes. She held out my belongings.

"You never let me come to the appointments, and I barely see any-one here. It's difficult to be indiscreet when there's no public appear-ances."

"But on the off chance we do have visitors, you still have to look the part."

"Ugh, fine." She pursed her lips.

Elisha could be defiant, but then, those feisty flames had kept her on my payroll and held me charmed for years.

It was why I kept her around. She amused me. In fact, she provided enough entertainment it warranted me saving her from a previous employer years ago. She also had a rather deviant sexual appetite, and after spending as much time together as we had…well, let's just say she provided more than typing services and calendar management.

I never had sussed out whether her extra office duties were performed out of duty, or desire. In the end, I didn't care either way. My job was stressful, and the occasional release eased the pressures of the position.

I had essentially bought out her contract from her last – owner – if you will. And for that act of kindness on my part, Elisha had developed deep loyalties toward me. Ties that had been tested over the years.

In my business, allegiances were rare.

But then, to be fair, Elisha's allegiance wasn't explicitly voluntary.

After all, being bound to me ensured she weighed each word I uttered, every motion I made, and the very emotion I portrayed very carefully.

One doesn't want to piss off the demon who owns the contract on your soul, now do they?

The drive over to my remote office – which really equated to nothing more than a cavernous empty hangar – relaxed me as I sat in the back of the Benz. Rodolfo navigated the precarious traffic.

I swished the bourbon and ice in the crystal tumbler, then took a sip. Chilled and rich, the amber liquid set the back of my mouth on fire.

"Busy day, Mr. Ronove?" Rodolfo inquired.

"As always."

"The QE-2 is backed up, again. It always is this time of day. Shall

3

I take an alternate route?" My secondary work area lay on the outskirts of the city in an industrial section. It's remote location made confidentiality easier.

"Please. I have to be there before three."

"Very well, sir."

I got lost in watching the scenery and the odd car zip by. Some we passed, others passed us. The drink in my hand decreased with each sip until all that remained were mishapen cubes. The car came to a slow stop.

Rodolfo opened his door, and stepped out.

The crunch of gravel under his leather patent shoes was a familiar sound, one I didn't like, and always put me on edge. I have a thing about noises. I prefer my surroundings to be relatively peaceful. Maybe it was just the familiar noise of the crunch, knowing what was coming next.

This particular part of my job wasn't my favorite. And eventually all my business dealings ended up here.

The car's door opened for me. I stepped out, leaving the empty glass sitting on the console. The grinding of stone on stone beneath my foot made me cringe as I walked to the hangar. Rodolfo, in the lead, got to the large door first, yanking on the handle so that the entire panel slid open.

It screeched open making me shudder as my skin turned to gooseflesh.

I stepped into the hangar.

Rodolfo slammed the large aluminium door shut, cutting himself off from me, and any daylight that had peeked through the open door into the massive area.

The vastness of the room before me, once briefly illuminated, plunged into darkness as the light from outside was cut sharply away.

It took a few moments of standing motionless before the heavy air inside the hangar settled me. My eyesight adjusted.

Off in the corner several candles with flickering flames were placed into the proper pattern.

Years of repeating this ritual had left an indellible mark on the cold cement floor.

A pentacle had been painted in goat's blood on the floor. Tall white tapers at each point of the star had been melted at the base so they stood firm. Their flames danced like strippers around unseen poles in some seedy men's club.

The scent of copper from the animal blood hung in the shadows. The head of the animal ripped from the body lay at the forefront of the inverted star. Dead eyes, milked over, stared at the ceiling.

A woman sat in the center of the pentagram. Bound, gagged and blindfolded, half-naked and shivering, her head swiveled in my direction as I stepped towards her.

As much as I disliked this task, a contract could only be sealed and completed after the signee had made their payment in full. I made my way toward her. The click of my soles against the concrete intensified her fear.

I could smell the dread. Humans sweat when they are terrified. A cold sweat. And its heady aroma is an aphrodesiac. Musky and sweet, it always makes my mouth water.

She whimpered.

There was a single, metal folding chair left there for me situated outside of the pentagram, near the decapitated goat's head.

I removed my tailored suit jacket, and hung it from a hook on the wall. Unbottoning my sleeves I cuffed each one. Loosening the tieknot by jerking it a few times back and forth, it relinquished it's tight grip and then I undid the fashionalbe noose. I hung the tie off the hook as well, then unbuttoned a couple of the shirt's top buttons, which removed the constant feeling of being choked.

I had learned over the years this last part could get messy, and I needed to be comfortable.

The girl let out a whine, as she bit into her gag. Sweat stains produced circles under her arms, and her clothes. What was left of her once trendy outfit, now hung in tatters from her body, ripped and sporting several stains.

I'd have to have a chat with Elisha. The hired help who collected my bounties when they were due had failed to carry out the smallest amount of class, leaving my asset in an unsavory condition.

A sheen of sweat glistened her forehead. I leaned over and snatched her blindfold off. Her eyes belayed the panick she must have been feeling, as her gaze darted back and forth. But there was no escape. Not now.

Perhaps before she had put her signature in her own blood on the parchment, but once I had an autograph, this current situation was unavoidable. Humans still haven't learned the power of knowing and having the name of a being. Especially once its written.

I sat down on the hard surface of the chair, bent over, and unsnapped my briefcase.

I extracted a single sheet of paper.

The contract was as clean and fresh as the day it had been signed. Exactly six years ago from today's date. The blood signature had dried quite dark. Even in the darkness of the cavernous warehouse, I could see the deep brown scrawl.

The girl began to cry. I glanced at the contract for the woman's name.

"Brie. Come now. You knew this was coming."

She wriggled, straining against the zipties that held her hands behind her back. Mascara ran down her face in inky rivulets.

"You had six highly successful years as a," I peered at the contract for a second time, " a model." I nodded and then shrugged. "Vapid choice, but each to their own. Looks like you made a tidy sum of money. I hope you had the forsight to leave a will so that someone inherits all those funds."

Brie chewed on her gag. She fought against the binds. A hundred years ago the frenetic last surge of energy that led a human to fight against their captor had been humorous. After seeing it so many times, it bored me.

Brie jerked her head up, still gnawing on the gag. She was trying to say something.

Shaking my head and rolling my eyes, I leaned over, and lowered the oily strip of torn fabric my hired help had used to ensure she wouldn't scream too loudly. The gag was covered in saliva.

I wiped my hand on my slacks.

Humans were sloppy things.

"I want more time." She cried.

"Oh, honey, it doesn't work that way." I reached out and placed my hand on her cheek. "Your payment to me, was your soul in exchange for six years of success. You received exactly what you asked for. It's time to pay up."

"But I have a daughter. She's only three." Her face scrunched up as the tears began again.

I glanced at my watch. Two-fifty five. Only a few more minutes.

"That's not really my concern."

Her face made that weird desperate frown I'd seen so often. Her eyes closed tight and her lips disappeared into a thin line. She hyper-ventilated it quick bursts, "Please…"

I stared at her.

"Please, I'll do anything." Begging was common.

I was never really sure what hellish beast would show up to take the payment. It all depended on the character of the vessel. This one was shallow, vain, and frantic which meant a lower lifeform would come to harness the soul. That also meant it would be messy.

The usual courier was a hellhound, but I've seen lamias, ghouls, wraiths and even a litch once. On the rarest of occasions, one of the lower demons from the pits would appear. When that happened, it was pretty much a guarantee the intended purpose of the reaping was to create a new demon. That's not the usual endgame.

I'd seen it happen throughout my stint. But not often, maybe a half dozen times.

You have to be one shady son of a bitch before the King of Hell is going to make you one of his own. The rest of these poor sots would end up as food. A soul is nothing more than the energy, the devine sub-stance that powers a human sac of flesh. Energy cannot be created nor destroyed, therefore, the soul is pure vitality.

Tasty human vigor.

And the consumption of a celestial entity can sustain a beast from the nether realm for years. Hence the contracts. It's been my job for hundreds of years.

Find food.

Or worthy bastards that can multiply our ranks.

So that's what I do.

I glanced at my watch. Two fifty-eight.

The candles fluttered as a breeze rolled across the smooth cold concrete. There was an undertone of rot in the gentle wind.

And in a single heartbeat, the cool breeze became ice cold.

My breath hung in the air before me as I exhaled.

"Say goodnight, Brie."

"No." She sobbed, "please!" She screamed.

Shadows in the corners of the hangar thickened. A growl rumbled throughout the space. Brie began openly wailing.

The growl announced hellhounds. Not surprising.

Funny thing. Souls are actually connected to the spine and the rib cage. Little energetic threads attach to the corporeal body to the heavenly spirit. Of course, only preternatural beings like myself can actually see the connection. Regardless, before Brie would see her final end, that connection to her mortal flesh had to be severed. That's why Death carries a scythe.

But when life is about to be interrupted, that separation needs to happen. And this is where it gets nasty.

The *click clack, click clack* of long sharp puppy nails echoed through the chamber. The air bit at my flesh like we were outside in a Canadian snowstorm. Brie continued her screams of terror.

Yellow eyes of the hellhound appeared. They glared at me.

I nodded and pointed at Brie.

The beast lunged, opening it's saliva dripping maw, exposing rows of sharp pointed teeth.

The first bite clamped down on the tender flesh of Brie's neck under the jaw. Blood sprayed in an arc, splattering across my chest.

"Damn it, I knew I shouldn't have worn this." The garment was ruined. I began to remove my shirt as the dog continued.

Brie spasmed and shrieked in pain.

The hound gnawed on her.

I swore the beast smiled as flesh ripped and bones crunched.

The next few minutes were a bloody mess. The mongrel tore Brie apart, separating those fragile little cords, freeing her soul from the flesh. As the spirit lifted unrestricted from the chunks of bloodied meat, the beast snapped at it, grabbing a floating limb, then scampered off into the darkness.

Blood pooled outward, obliterating the pentagram on the floor and running beneath the severed goat's head.

Well, that was done. I wiped my sullied hands on my pants.

I'd have people come in and clean this up. We had ways of disposing of the body so that nothing was ever found.

Holding up the contract, still unspoiled, it ignited.

Smoldering and sparking, the flames of hell crawled up the sheet, eating the paper, casting flickering shadows against the walls. I felt the intense hellflame heat against my bare chest. I held the paper out a little further. Last thing I wanted was singed chest hair.

As the flames crawled closer to my fingers I dopped the now useless document. The contract had been fulfilled and was no longer required. Of course, I retained copies. For accounting purposes.

Swaying back and forth the paper traversed through the ice cold air currents of my remote office.

As the contract hit the concrete, what was left combusted and burned bright consuming the remanants of the paper. And then darkness fell in the hangar again. The chill subsided and the nether realm's shadows recoiled back into the corners.

Time to get another deal on the books.

Grabbing my coat and tie from the hook where they hung, I tucked them under my arm, careful not to get the lavish suit material anywhere near my bloody shirt clasped in my other hand.

Rodolfo was waiting for me, car door open, standing at attention.

"Went well, sir?" He handed me a fresh shirt.

"As expected."

"Usual clean up crew?"

"Please." I tossed my jacket and tie into the backseat, then buttoned up the new shirt. I didn't bother tucking it in. I was going home.

And those were the last words uttered. Silence at last. Rodolfo drove me back to my downtown penthouse apartment.

PART 2

Dominic Ronove
Friday, 8:46pm

Hot water cascaded down my back, bouncing off my shoulders and spraying onto the tiled shower stall. As the water flowed from the shower head and pooled around my feet, I couldn't help but think of Brie.

Fangs. Growls. Blood. Lots of flowing blood.

Hundreds of years. One more contract. Another lost soul.

It never ends.

And with the completion of the pact this afternoon, there were expectations of another to be lined up. It didn't matter how many I had in the bank, or that three more in the next week would meet the same fate.

The water in my shower would never run cold, unlike Brie's blood. Not in this condo which I paid far too much to keep. But then I got remunerated handsomely for perpetually supplying the fiends of the world below. I forced myself to shut the water off.

Time to go to work.

Within a short few minutes, I was dressed in well fitted jeans, a tight t-shirt and my favorite pair of cowboy boots.

My style may have shocked some, colleagues particularly, but not if they knew me well, and few did. Everyone expected a contract demon to be forever donned in black, but I had learned a long time ago to dress for the occasion.

If I wanted to get close to humans, have them trust me, I needed to dress like them.

And what better place to go to find the depressed, the needy, and the desperate?

A bar.

I knew just the right place. A drinking establishment I frequented a few times a week. It attracted everyone. Men, women, professionals, blue collar, straight, gay and everything in between. Oddly enough, it was called *The Common*, and the name couldn't have been a more perfect fit, for its patrons were exactly that. Common. The owners, not so much. But the customers were a dime a dozen, the rank and file of the human lot.

Inevitably, someone would be lamenting on a bar stool soaked in one too many cocktails or brews. And that was usually my best place to initiate a transaction.

Keep in mind, getting someone to sign over their soul was rarely a one visit, stop and shop deal.

It required finesse, smooth talking, identified commonalities, developed trust and occasionally a few lies. Little white lies. Think of it as the ultimate seduction. A warm smiling face. Nods of acceptance and understanding. A gentle squeeze of the hand when they first open up, or a pat on the back. Depending on the personality, sometimes a round of shots is required. Mutual inebriation to celebrate their misery.

Which is how I step in and tell them how I can make it all better. If for only a short while.

Six years. That's all they ever get.

Of course, there are exceptions. Elisha and Rodolfo being a couple notable cases, but then their lives are devoted to complete servitude. And I continue to renew their contracts as long as their loyalties remain intact.

But now I have a free space. An empty spot of my shelf.

One contract completes, another is one is expected.

"Hey Sung," I parked myself at the end of the bar, noddding to the bartender.

"Dom. Usual?" Sungjin wasn't the owner. From first appearances, you'd never guess, but Sung was a couple hundred years old, and *The Common* was a bit of a front. The bar was a cover, a rather propserous one at that, but a cover, nonetheless.

Sungjin was the scout for a coven of vampires.

It had taken a few decades to work out a system of trust, and acceptance between myself and the *Basrahip*, the high priest. This particular coven had a long history and tradition that reached back to Turkey. Of course it wasn't known as Turkey when the *Basrahip* had been reborn as the undead. No, Turkey had been the Ottoman Empire. But as ancient creatures go, we keep certain traditions and names while still managing to move forward with the times.

Anonymity is essential. Tradition, however, is eternal.

Given the rather dubious nature of our existence, being unseen ensures we stay alive, or undead...whatever. It's complicated.

Sung placed a tumbler in front of me. The caramel aroma, with just a hint of apple wafted from the glass.

I pulled my wallet out.

Sung held up his hand, "Working tonight?"

"Of course. When am I not?"

Sung snorted, "True enough. This one's on me. Just lay low? Sahir is on a tear about the lack of available sustenance."

"He's rather particular though, no?" I picked up the tumbler, tipped it towards Sung in thanks, then sipped the amber liquid.

I closed my eyes, concentrating on the multitude of flavors dancing in my mouth. Of course, the caramel was most prominent, it was also the most aromatic. But there were hints of honey, apple, oak, and cloves.

Dare I say, heavenly? Best not.

"Yes, Sahir likes his food, shall we say, immature. Developed, but not experienced in everything life has to offer."

"Virgins?" I arched an eyebrow.

"Not necessarily, just perhaps not so...polluted." Sung said the last word almost under his breath. He glanced around the bar.

I caught his meaning.

In the last hundred years, humans had advanced quickly. And with that, the lust for experiences and growing up meant that finding anyone in their mid twenties who was still naïve, and unfamiliar with the ways of the world was a virtual impossibility. Humans wanted to taste everything, and most were oblivious or blatantly ignorant to apparent dangers. Alcohol, drugs, and sex, all kinds of sex, were sought after and generally obtained. But all those experiences left markers in the body.

You're all tainted.

Sahir must be starving. And a hungry vampire is a testy creature.

15

Sung's request meant no ruckus in the bar tonight, no contract signing, no sliding off into the shadows with a human. No, best to keep the peace. Tonight would be all about reconnaisance.

Nodding to Sung, understanding the predicament, I would keep to my best behavior. Like I said, it had taken decades of careful negotiation in order to even step foot in this bar. I wasn't going to ruin a well honed relationship.

I swiveled my bar stool around, surveying the occupants. A young woman spied me from across the room. Surrounded by heavy conversation with a small group of friends, she barely paid them any mind. All her attention was on me.

There's a certain type of personality that can sniff out bad energy and that same type is also instantly attracted to it. Guaranteed those humans don't live long lives. They tend to make a consecutive string of poor life choices. Some of them end up in my hands.

And here she comes. About to make yet another seriously bad move.

I wasn't going to stop her.

Her red dyed hair was voluminous, as were her curves. I have always appreciated a curvy woman. Societal epxectations of beauty have changed many times over the course of my long lifetime. As much as I try to move with the current trends, some proclivities are rooted deep in my history.

She sidled right up to me, making no bones about her intentions, her hip snuggling right up against my thigh. She waved down Sung and asked for two shots of tequila.

"You want lime and salt too, hun?" Sung asked. His gaze flicked to me. I shrugged and gave him an *I didn't do anything* look. I'd known him long enough to know by his look that he was laughing on the inside, but

16

also reminding me of tonight's rules.

"No thanks. I like it raw." She winked at Sung, then slid one shot glass over to me. "No fun drinking this by myself and my friends are about to leave. I'm just starting to get riled up. Get riled up with me."

"All right. What's your name?"

"Amber."

"Of course it is." I replied, with a genuinely devilish smile.

"You're hot." She ran the tips of her fingers over my shoulder and down the front of my chest.

Truthfully, taking this vuluptuous female home and fucking the hell out of her, all the puns intended, would have been a fun evening. But I needed a contract, not a tussle in the sheets. There was a possibility here, but she lacked a certain amount of desperation.

Humans who smell like burnt black pepper; those are the ones I'm looking for. That aroma is desperation. Those are easy contracts. Amber wasn't there. Give her another five years, and a solid succession of bad decisions and she'd be ready. Amber was someone I needed to keep an eye on, but she wasn't ready, not yet.

"Sung!" A gruffish voice barreled through the bar, near the entrance. A gaggle of young men had entered. The one who had bellowed the bartender's name led the pack. Late twenties? Maybe? Both ears pierced with tiny gold hoops, a strong chin, covered in light brown stubble, and a row of perfectly white teeth. A scar ran through an eyebrow, evident by the missing hair.

"Mal, my man, how's it going?" Sung did a strange coordinated handshake with gestures and fist pumps in the air with this Mal.

"It's Friday!"

"The usual?" Sung inquired.

"You bet! For the gang!"

Sung turned toward the bar and began pulling draught and mixing shots.

Mal glanced over at my direction, and for the briefest of moments, I would have sworn the world slowed as he stared. I couldn't tell if his eyes had pierced my human meat sack and saw the fiend beneath. Was this a glance of recognition? I had never seen this creature, Mal, before. And then his gaze shifted, as if he *knew* what I was. A flash. Nothing more, then it was gone, replaced with a beaming smile. He gave me a curt nod and bit of a smirk.

I squinted, studying him, then returned the gesture, but my nod back was a little more deliberate and longer in action.

"Oh, so you like the boys." Amber was still standing beside me. I had forgot all about her and her tequila shot.

I laughed, "He's pretty good looking, wouldn't you say?"

Amber almost smiled, she was forcing herself not to. Leaning over my shoulder, intentionally pressing her breasts against me, she took a long look at the bar's newest arrival.

"Actually, he is kind of delicious." She rubbed herself against me.

"Yes, he is."

"How about both of us?" She whispered in my ear, then gently nibbled my lobe.

I pulled her around so I could glare at her, "Well, if you think you can net him and bring him over here, sure."

"A challenge. I like it. Don't move. I'll be back."

Amber disappeared into the crowd. It was Friday night, the place was filling up. It took several minutes, and a few sips of my drink before I spotted her again. She had Mal pressed up against the back wall. From where I sat, she was giving one hell of a sales pitch.

I've been around a long time. I think I've come to know humans

18

rather well.

Mal was about as likely to take her up on her offer as a rat would have been willing to crawl in front of a hungry snake who was coiled and ready to strike. But, good on her for trying.

I chuckled to myself, repositioned myself on my barstool, and glanced at the patrons coming and going around me. Each one got the sniff test looking for that black pepper of desperation.

My glass was almost empty, and I was about to summon Sung for another when a hand clasped my shoulder.

I don't like being touched. At least, not without an invite. The fires of rage burst into a bonfire. I clenched my jaw, pushing down my ire. I could feel the air around me darken.

Sung felt it too, and gave me a warning glare.

Remembering our earlier conversation, I reigned it all in, and turned my head slightly.

It was Mal.

That altered everything. His eyes were stunning. The lightest of brown. Damn near gold. If I had to name them, I'd say topaz, but with just hints of green. Regardless, they were so light in color with a kohl edge they seemed impossibly human.

"Hey, I'm Malik. My friends call me Mal." He stuck out his hand.

Like I said, I don't like people touching me, usually, but those who make poor decisions, or who ramp up my sexual appetites will some-times get a pass. With human traditions, like handshakes, I had to sometimes forgo my preferences and make exceptions.

I swung my barstool around, and returned the gesture, clasping Mal's warm fleshy palm.

"Dom."

"Thanks for sending your girlfriend over. That was quite the invitation."

"Oh, she's not my girlfriend. Don't even remember her name."

"For someone you don't remember, she suggested some rather wild activities for the night. Just thought I'd come over and say thanks, but, not really into the threesomes with girls. Now, if you ever want to go solo –"

"Never said I wouldn't be interested in that."

"Well, really now." Mal raised an eyebrow.

I liked him.

There was no black pepper. Not a hint of it. But he was cocky, unbelievably handsome, and confident. I liked confidence in suitors. If you had the balls to approach a demon, you had a good set of knackers. I suspected Mal's were big.

Don't get me wrong. I'd met my fair share of women who had big balls too. Lady balls. Often the women outmatched the men. But something about Mal made me want to see how low hanging his junk really was.

"Let me buy you another." Mal offered while his eyes enthralled me.

I was about to agree to his attempt to seduce me.

When the entire bar flooded with white light.

Blinding white light.

And that only meant one thing.

It didn't happen very often. Not many humans were capable of pulling it off.

Some asshole was summoning me. I fought the blinding light off through furrowed brows and intense concentration, but I needed to act fast. A beckoning meant my body would dematerialize from where I was, and pop into existence where ever the ritual was taking place. I couldn't very well do that in the middle of a crowded bar.

"Ah, shit." I flipped my wrist to look at my watch. "Look, I actually have to go. Maybe another time."

I pulled my wallet out, took out a couple of twenties and left them tucked under the tumbler glass for Sung. Then I took out a business card and left it on the bar.

I tapped my finger on it, "If you think you're still willing to attempt your seduction another night, give me a call."

Stepping off the barstool, and grabbing my jacket, I headed to the door.

I hadn't barely got into the back alley behind *The Common* when the blinding light consumed me.

The flames of hell scorched and licked every fiber of my body. I hated being summoned.

It hurt like hell.

Instantly put me into a foul mood.

Pulled across the barriers of space doesn't feel great either.

In a heartbeat I stood in some rural location. An intersection.

A crossroads.

And standing in the middle of the road was a disheveled middle-aged man, looking like shit, like he hadn't slept in a week. A pentagram had been scratched into the gravel and dirt at his feet, and he was surrounded by a giant circle lined with salt.

"That's not going to protect you, idiot. Salt is for ghosts."

Honestly, the amount of rumor and myth was astounding. Which was a good thing. The red herrings and misinformation out in the world clouded the actual facts. Obscuring how to call me meant this kind of an encounter was a rarity.

The idiot pointed at the protective ring, "Yes it will. The book said so."

"Don't believe everything you read." I glared at the man. Time to pull hell up from the depths, release the beast, so to speak. My eyes flooded with light as the pupils expanded. I knew from a human's perspective, it appeared as if the entire eyeball went black. Trick of the light and shadow. But with my demonic eyes, my extra sensory ability triggered. I could see everything. Thoughts, emotions, history, knowledge. It allowed me access to everything I required to ensare a human. To twist words into lies, to make falsehoods seem plausible.But the minute I glared at the summoner with demon eyes, I knew this situation was entirely different.

PART 3

I gripped my beer bottle tightly, to the point where my knuckles were white.

Heaving a sigh, I put one hand out and caught the edge of the bar to steady myself. I'd never approached or been as forward with anyone as I'd been with the dark and handsome man who'd called himself Dom.

"Blew you off too, huh?" Turning my head toward the voice, Amber, the girl with the naughty invitation had taken up residence beside me. She had a sneer on her face as she glanced longingly at the exit to the bar where Dom had left. "Man, I thought for sure I was gonna get laid." Then she tilted her head up and glared at me with a wanting look.

"No, no way sister. That's not happening." I held my hand. "Not that you aren't gorgeous, 'cause you are, but I don't play for your team."

"Well, a girl's gotta try." Amber shrugged her shoulders.

"Sorry to disappoint. Tell you what, let me buy you a drink. It won't replace getting laid, but if you can't get fucked, get fucked up." I waved down Sung.

"Oh, I like that. Okay, I will take that drink." Amber placed her empty cocktail glass on the bar. Sung wasted no time in making another for her and handed it to Amber. I gave Sung my last twenty. I groaned a little at the realization I'd have to use my credit card for the rest of the night.

"Here's to getting messy." We raised our drinks in a mutual toast to the evening's celibacy. "Come meet my friends." Sung returned with my change, which I pocketed, but after leaving a couple of bucks on the bar top as a tip.

Amber studied me closely, then nodded. "Sure, why the hell not. Are they all —?"

"Yes. Screaming queens, every last one of them."

"Well damn. Do they at least dance?"

"Until the bar closes. Let's go have some fun and forget about the one that got away."

"I like you. You're fun." Amber slid her hand over my shoulder as we made our way to the dance floor heading toward waving arms from a group of men who were obviously calling us over to their cluster.

Except I couldn't quite shake the image of the one who walked away. Tall, dark, brooding, handsome as hell, but oddly unnerving. I would have said he was my perfect fantasy, but there was something else. Something I couldn't quite figure out.

Just for reassurance, I stuck my hand in my pocket and lightly fingered the card Dom had left. I needed to know it was still there.

The coat check line wasn't too bad, but then it was late summer, and the most anyone lugged around was a light jacket, if anything at all. The collection of miscreants I called my friends had slowly dwindled over the course of the night, until it was just me, Amber and my roommate Scott.

After waiting for Amber to retrieve her purse – which was more of a piece of luggage – we exited the bar and started walking toward Scott's car.

"Are you guys hungry?" I asked. "I could eat."

"I'm always down to eat." Scott's eyes went wide. At one point, Scott and I had tried the dating thing. He was gorgeous. Shoulder length thick dirty blonde hair, a regular at the gym, several days' worth of stubble with his chin whiskers kept extra-long. His close-cropped beard was mottled, with patches of platinum streaks nestled in an autumn days' worth of brown. In the sunlight, there were even highlights of red. But despite my physical attraction, the relationship game hadn't really worked out well. Instead, we decided we were way better as friends.

On the rare occasion, Scott would slip into my bed, or I his, especially when a few weeks had passed with no interesting prospects from our frequent nights on the town, or even trolling on the hook-up apps. Nothing serious ever came out of our romps. It was all fun.

A relationship between the two of us would never have worked. Scott wanted to be able to see others, and that didn't sit well with me. I didn't think there was anything wrong with open relationships, it just wasn't something I wanted for myself. And besides, both Scott and I were more geared for receiving. We both wanted pitchers. Scott also had a bizarre passion for the woods, hiking, camping and outdoor activity – which is most likely why he looked so rugged and handsome. All that rock climbing and kayaking kept his body as fit as it was. Lean, taught, furry and fit.

I had no interest in the outdoors. I still tried to get exercise, but I was more comfortable with a book in my hand than an oar, or some sporting equipment.

So, friends it was, with the occasional make out session.

"Food sounds good. I need something to soak up this alcohol. Do you know of anything nearby that's still open this late?" Amber questioned us.

I glanced at Scott and grinned, "The Greasy Spoon!" We said in unison and then laughed.

I turned back to Amber and explained, "It was the first restaurant Scott and I went to together on a date."

"Wait, you two—?" Amber's glance bounced between us.

"At one point we tried." Scott laughed. "We're better as friends."

"Wow, I wish my exes were as cool."

"I'm not sure you'd call us exes. More like incompatible romantically but still good friends. Besides, he's usually gone most of the summer traipsing through the woods." I rolled my eyes.

"True." Scott nodded.

"Then what are you doing in the city?"

"I needed a shower. So bad."

"Also true." I grimaced. "When you walked in, I swore it smelled like you'd rolled in something dead."

Scott laughed.

"Okay, so, The Greasy Spoon it is."

"Is it good?" Amber asked.

"No. But who cares." Scott laughed.

The three of us drunk ate. Two bacon cheeseburgers and one chicken shawarma. A massive plate of fries sat in the center of the table with the intent all three of us would share the side order, but Scott ploughed through them.

"God, I wish I could eat fries like that and still look like you." Amber shook her head.

"He never sits down for more than five minutes. Drives me insane." I explained.

"I like to stay busy." Scott dipped a fry into some mayonnaise and then popped it into his mouth. I had called him out many times in the past for his choice in dipping sauce. He said it was his German heritage coming through. His grandmother had taught him.

"So, after your dad died?" I asked. Amber being new, had prompted the obligatory "And who are you and where did you come from" conversation. She had had a difficult childhood with tension and strife filling every nook and cranny of the family home. Her father battled depression and a never-ending string of jobs gained and lost. Her mother hadn't known how to deal with the bouts of sadness that turned her husband into a bedridden shell of a human. In the end, she gave up, and started drinking.

Amber landed the role as the scapegoat for her father's mental illness.

"Mom drank. More than ever. She always had a cocktail or two, you know? Maybe a little more than most people, but then she got nasty, and angry. And me being me, I got mouthy. The wrong choice of words and it was a slap across the face. Until she decided that wasn't enough punishment, and a slap turned into her fist. That's when I threw in the towel. I mean, she's my mom, right? I shoulda stuck around and helped her figure things out. But after my third trip to the emergency room, one of the nurses pulled me aside and gave me a number for a safe house. I didn't look back.

"Ten years later, here I am. A shitty job, an even shittier apartment and in desperate search for a man that's not like my father. I don't know if you've noticed, but I'm not having much luck." Amber ran her finger over the rim of her soda glass staring absently into the vessel.

"You make due and hope things get better. Scott and I haven't exactly had it easy either, but we've always had each other. Almost, anyway."

"How long have you two known each other?" Amber broke her stare and studied both Scott and Malik's faces.

Scott chuckled, "Forever." He turned, glancing at me, then elbowed my ribs.

"Seems like it." I rolled my eyes. "We have our own sob story too. We lived next door to each other and grew up together. Our parents were the best of friends. We basically had two sets of parents and two homes where we grew up.

"But then one night it all went to hell. Our parents got a babysitter to look after the two of us, and the grownups went out to have a good time. They never made it home. Drunk driver. Bad crash. No one survived. We went into the system and got split up. Then by a stroke of luck, found each other at eighteen and bonded together again like we'd never been apart.

"So, shitty, but not that bad." Scott smiled as he looked at me.

Amber's gaze went back and forth between the two men. "You guys are cute."

"We know." We said in unison. All three of us laughed.

"Not as cute as Dom though." Amber got in a jab. "That man was stunning."

"Yeah, he definitely was god-like, but ..." I lost any words to keep the conversation going as I recalled shaking the guy's hand. His skin was unusually cool to the touch, but there was strength in his grip. The skin-to-skin contact sent shivers down my spine and made my tummy do a funny flip-flop. Even thinking about it now, I felt odd. Off. I couldn't really discern the emotions.

It was eerie sensation. Not one I'd ever felt before and couldn't decide if I was attracted or terrified.

No one I've ever met had ever evoked such a strange combination of emotions.

Growing increasingly silent and distant I gazed out the window I sat next to and stared out into the darkness of the night beyond the restaurant. The depths of the shadows in the parking lot were as dark as Dom's thick beard and trimmed, in-style, manicured-to-perfection, fade haircut. The top locks had been left longer and had a gentle wave. His eyes were as black as night.

I shifted in the booth and pulled my jacket over my lap, as nonchalantly as possible to hide a growing erection.

"So, are you gonna call him?" Amber broke the uncomfortable silence. Scott continued to eat the few remaining fries left on the community plate, but his non-interested look didn't fool me. Scott had that "I'm not jealous, definitely jealous" look.

"I don't know." I let the last word trail off.

Should I?

"You totally should call him. And then after you go out on a date with him and let him fuck your brains out, you're going to call me and

29

tell me every single last detail." Amber bit her bottom lip. Obviously, the thought of two guys getting it on, got her off.

"You're a kinky bitch, aren't you?"

"Dude, you have no idea." Amber's eyes got wide for a second as she bit her bottom lip again but this time in a suggestive lascivious look, and then grinned. The facial expression was laced with mischievousness.

"Okay, you two. Barf." Scott chimed in.

But again, his obvious display of *I don't care* didn't ring true. It was cute, and I loved the fact that he was so protective of me. But if I didn't know any better, I would say he was being weirdly jealous. And for someone who purported to want an open relationship with any future husband, I didn't understand what was going on with him.

"Call him. Please, call him. I need you to get laid so I can live vicariously through you. I just know he's got a big dick. But I need details. Preferably pictures." Amber had grabbed my hand and squeezed it. "Do it. Please. For me."

"That is truly the most bizarre thing I've ever heard." Scott shook his head.

"Okay, I'll call him. For you, Amber."

PART 4

Dominic Ronove

Saturday, 1:34am

"Who the hell are you, and what kind of an entity are you working for?" I grabbed the suited man by the lapels of his coat and pulled him towards me.

The stench of a grave poured into my nostrils clotting in the back of my throat. It was sticky like mucous. Death has an unmistakable and resilient odor. It is thick and clings to everything. I would be lucky if a heavy washing would rid these clothes of the putrid scent.

But with my enhanced vision engaged, my extra sensory sight gave me flashes. Images of what had happened to this human.

A massive stroke.

A funeral home with handfulls of crying family members.

The inside of a casket, the lining smooth and satiny to the touch. The sound of shovel-fulls of dirt hitting the lid of the coffin tumbled around in my head, like I was hearing it from a 1930's gramaphone recording.

This man was dead.

The dead *can't* summon me.

"I'll only ask you one more time. Who or what are you working for?"

"I...I don't understand!" The corpse pulled away from me, took a step back and grabbed his head. He yanked at his hair, which came out in clumps. "I'm only doing what I was told."

"What were you told?"

"They made me. Don't you see? I can't help it. They made me." He began hitting himself.

Well this is just grand.

The summoning ritual had been performed by a corpse. That was something I'd never seen before. But it also didn't make sense. Something with a functioning brain had to perform the incantation, otherwise it wouldn't work. A soul is devine energy, and the brain is inextricably tied to and in communication with the spirit. The brain has the ability to call out to the devine in the soul, and through that contact collect electrical energy from the surrounding area and from within itself. If you're properly trained, you can harness the energy, program it with your intentions, then redirect it.

So you have to have a brain, in part, to call me. Of course the tantalizing morsel for me is a soul to bind. After all, if I show up and there's no reward there will be hell to pay. Literally.

This empty shell lacked the cantelope to summon me and the juicy spectral body for me to barter with.

So, a dead body couldn't possibly –

I was in a trap. A setup. A fucking ambush.

Glancing around the area's perimeter, I searched, reaching out with all my senses, trying to glean who had put this ill thought plan into motion. The corpse hadn't initiated the pentagram's inherent ability to keep me contained. A simple sigil wouldn't lock me in place. But the inverted star with the right set of words? Yup – that would lock me up good.

But that hadn't happened.

"All right, fucker. You want to play with a demon? That generally doesn't end well for humans."

There was a rustle at the base of a tree at the southwest corner of the crossroad.

The dead thing continued to beat itself up. It was ripping chunks of rotting flesh and hair and tossing them into the air. Body parts rained down on the gravel road.

Inhaling deeply, a lingering scent of live humans infiltrated my nose. Sickly sweet. There was a hint of fresh leaves in the air, like the budding of trees in Spring. That's excitement.

"I can smell you! Shall I sniff you out? Is that what you want? A child's game of hide and seek? Tell you what. Let's play. If I find you, then I get to drag you to hell." I growled.

Following my nose it didn't take long to find a spot where there had recently been a human male. But they weren't there now.

As I got closer, a vortex began to form from the stagnant water in the ditch. It climbed with every spiral, within seconds there was a writhing and twisting waterspout.

I heard something behind me. I spun around. Swirls of loose grass, little twigs and dust cycloned across the dirt road. A whilwind of earth. A dust devil.

"Shit!" This wasn't good. This was elemental magic. And only one type of creature was capable of harnessing this energy. White witches.

I turned again, just to my left, a small vortex of air was approaching. Fire was all that was missing. Generally, none of these things on its own would harm me. Together, it might play havoc with the body I'd been lugging around for a couple of hundred years. It was a good flesh suit. The poor sot I had taken it from had been fraught with life's stresses. No job, a family to feed, a misunderstanding with the local law enforcement. The last thing I wanted was to have my physical body damaged. It was a handsome shell, and I had grown accustomed to it. Besides, healing wounds in a borrowed body presented its own set of complications.

The confused corpse was still staggering around the inside of the pentagram that had been constructed to summon me. It plunged one hand into its stomach making an audible *squish*. With a violet yank, it pulled out one of those transfusion plastic bags full of blood, sealed with a cap on top. The zombie bit on the cap and ripped it off. It started pouring the blood overtop of the salt that defined the five pointed star.

"Damnit." Salt will protect a human from the spirit world, but iron has the ability to contain me. And human blood has enough iron to do exactly that. It won't physically harm me, but it locks me into or out of a place if the right sigils are used. And blood can be used as a replacement for the right spell words.

Fuck.

Whoever was behind this knew what to do – to hell with all the misinformation.

If the gaggle of witches performing this hoodoo managed to get me in the centre of that pentagram, and completed the right scripts with a human blood circle around me, while keeping me guarded with the elemental whirlwinds, I was fucked.

Meddlesome bitches. There were three covens in the city I knew of, and I had tangled with each of them, more than once. Those bitches were a constant thorn in my side.

But this was all new. I hadn't sensed this style or flavour of magic before.

My last serious go-round hadn't happened with white witches in at least a hundred years. Black witches, constantly. White, they were a rarity. With the development of human endeavors, science, mechanics, and industrialism, the realm of magic and faith in such primal forces had melted away like a waning moon.

Modern day witches lacked the ability to tap into more ancestral magic because of their reliance on societies advancements. But this current situation had me second guessing that assumption.

Fuck. Fuck. Fuck.

I had to think back. I haven't survived for as long as I have without knowing how to navigate through the realm of the supernatural. Magic always left traces. A fingerprint if you will. And every spell had a unique signature. A human moniker.

Humans who had an exceptional tie to divinity, mind you, but still they were all baseless and dirty humans.

The swirling columns of elemental magic were backing me up into the pentagram.

The zombie had finished half the circle by pouring its surprise bag of blood overtop of the salt. The sigils it had written were crude, but it would work. I needed to destroy the writing, but I also needed to know *who* was doing this.

It shoved its hand inside itself again and pulled out another bag, ripping off the top with black and rotting teeth. As he poured the glistening red liquid, I grabbed the dead thing and pulled him toward me.

Blood sprayed everywhere. My second shirt of the day became

35

splattered and subsequently ruined.

Baring my fangs and opening my mouth I lunged towards the corpse, grabbed him by the neck and wrenched him toward me.

I sank my teeth into his face, ripping off a good chunk of it's cheek. As I chewed the rotting flesh, flashes of information were supplied. I was hunting for that signature. The leftover thumbprint.

Again, after living for hundreds of years roaming topside, I can read the tiniest fractions of residual magic. By extrapolating the images I can get a pretty intact scenario. History repeats itself, and humans aren't that complicated. Patterns are a thing.

There were three of them. Siblings. Two men, one woman. All in their early twenties. The boys were weak in comparison to the girl. The girl had come into her power with grace and ease. The boys struggled with it.

I glanced around my immediate surroundings while the zombie thrashed to get loose from my grip. I was almost certain the witches were close.

"Bitch, you can't beat me!" I screamed into the night air. The zombie continued to fight. Its rotting cheek flesh squished between my teeth. With another chew, my teeth hit a pocket of rot which gushed black ooze. It tasted foul. Horrid enough I couldn't keep my mouth closed. The festering liquid trickled over my lips and down my chin.

"Mmhmm. Your not that strong, hell fiend." I heard the taunt. The voice was distinctly feminine, like a whisper in the night breeze. There was no fear, no second-guessing. The female witch was over-confident, and I would guess scrying to witness the current situation from some distant hidden sanctuary. I sensed her magic. A tingle under the skin.

A vehicle's headlights appeared in the distance. A cloud of dust billowing out behind it. It was approaching at an alarming rate, and speeding up as it came careening towards me and the zombie. As it approached, the witch's puppet continued to wave around the second bag of blood, sloshing blood all over the place. But he was making a surprising amount of coverage and the circle was nearly intact.

Shit.

As the car came within a few meters of the crossroads, it spun to the side and came to a gravel scattering stop. The skid from the tires pelted us with little stones. I turned away from the rock storm, letting go of the zombie and shielded my face. Last thing I wanted were a bunch of cuts and scrapes.

Despite the pebble onslaught and the risk to my flesh, the car's skid obliterated one side of the circle.

My escape.

The driver's door opened.

It was Rodolfo.

And he came brandishing a shotgun. He flipped the beast of a weapon onto the roof of the car, tucked the butt into his shoulder, bent over and squinted through the gun's scope while he aimed.

From out of the witch's dust devil, large stones and branches came hurtling towards us.

"Duck." Rodolfo instructed.

I didn't need to be told twice. I hit the dirt and covered my head with my hands.

A loud *bang* shattered the countryside with its noise.

Tiny *thump thump thumps* rained down on top of me.

A larger *thump* followed as the animated dead thing fell on top of me.

I opened my eyes and lifted my head, trying to look around me.

The funnels of magic slowly died, spinning into nothingness.

With one yank Rodolfo was pulling the lifeless dead weight off of me, and then hauled me up onto my feet.

"You okay, boss?"

Rodolfo brushed some of the dirt off my shoulders, but I was covered in gravel, decayed body bits and blood soaked salt crystals. Black ooze from the zombie's cheek I had still tucked inside my mouth coated my tongue and palate. I spit the hunk out, and tried to get as much of the putrid taste out as well. Pieces of of rotting flesh that confettied my hair fell to my feet.

"Ah, boss?"

"What?" I was not happy.

"You got a problem." He pointed at my upper arm.

A good sized stick had nestled deep into my deltoid.

"This has been a shit show of a night." I balled my fists up and shook with fury. "Fucking witches!" But it wasn't Rodolfo's fault. If anything, he'd just saved my ass.

"Let me just—" Rodolfo put on hand on the front of my shoulder, grasped the embedded branch and yanked.

"Fucking, hell!" I screamed.

"We'll get you patched up."

"Take me home Rodolfo." Healing me was more complicated than you'd think.

"Yes, boss."

The ride home was deathly silent, but only a few minutes into the ride I had to lower the backseat windows. I couldn't stand the smell wafting off of me.

The smell of death.

I was going to enjoy exterminating these witches.

No, that's too quick.

I had to come up with something far more devious.

The next day I had calmed down considerably, but it had taken me hours to wash off the dead zombie parts that had managed to find themselves in rather unusual places. The sticky tar that had coated my mouth and throat had the taste of moldy food and spoiled milk. There wasn't enough mouthwash in the entire city to rid my tastebuds of the revolting flavor.

I had discovered several cuts and of course, the puncture in my arm from the wayward tree limb. The wound didn't really weap blood. After all the body I inhabited was dead. My demonic energy powered it. So the one thing I desperately didn't want to have happen, happened anyway. Now I'd need to perform a healing ritual to stitch the flesh back together.

I rolled my eyes and shook my head at the thought of having to carry out *that* paticular ritual. Magic tends to fall into two camps. Angelic or demonic. Healing obviously fell into the camp I didn't belong to, therefore my hesitation.

But the task would have to happen sooner rather than later. I could have found another human host, but two things prevented me from doing so. Contracts I was currently working on or had nearly wrapped up wouldn't recognize a new meat suit. And not every human body can contain demonic energy. Some burn out too fast. This body held onto my energies. We synergized right from the get-go. It was a good match. And like I've said – the human who had once inhabited this flesh was a handsome fucker. I liked my look. The dark features matched my personality.

"You're getting careless with your meat sack," I mumbled to myself as I wrapped my wound. The fixing of this would have to wait until later.

After several cups of coffee and a hefty breakfast, I swear I could still taste the rotted zombie in my mouth.

I had Rodolfo drive me back out to the crossroads where the disastrous evening had taken place. I knew what I was looking for, but tracking them down was going to require a truly diabolical effort.

As the car rolled to a stop, I swung the back door open, and stepped out into the daylight. The sun was warm and intensely bright. I adjusted my sunglasses, pushing them up closer to my eyes. Thank the depths I wasn't limited to a time of day, unlike my friend Sung at *The Common*. There was no sunrise or daylight strolls in his future. Ever.

I knelt down in front of the pentagram's remanants, inhaled, trying to catch wind of anything I might of missed last night.

But there was nothing.

"Rodolfo?"

His door swung open. He was extremely tall, towering well above the car's roof as he straighted himself coming to attention as I beckoned him. He took a few steps around to the passenger side of the car and opened the door.

"Get out." Rodolfo barked.

A young man, early twenties, inebriated beyond reason, fell out of the car.

"Just place him in what's left of this circle." I instructed.

Rodolfo grabbed the waistband of his jeans and the front of the man's hoodie and picked him up like a sack of potatoes. With as much effort as slinging said bag of vegetables, he tossed the man into the center of the circle.

"Good. Grab me a strip of the corpse's clothes." Rodolfo returned a moment later and handed me the front lapel of the dead man's suit. Its headless body lay by the side of the road.

Our intoxicated friend, who despite the dried puke splattered across his stomach and jeans, would have been kinda cute. His light brown hair hung listlessly in front of his brown eyes. Eyes that were dead. The spark had gone out of them long ago.

"Geeze, Rodolfo. How much sedative did you give him? He's a fucking mess."

"Lots. I hate it when they fight. Or squirm."

This pickled excuse for a man was a archetypical example of a sloppy human.

Unable to cope, or adult, I'd had this one on my list to sign to contract for the past year. Constantly stoned or drunk, never in their right mind, and perpetually angry, it was only a matter of time before he'd land himself in a situation where he'd require my help. His head lolled to one side as he gazed up at me.

"Where 'm I?" He slurred.

"You're about to go home. For good."

"You're kinda hot." For a moment, I thought he was going to puke the way he started gagging on his own words. But like most who chose to live in a state of constant intoxication, he recovered, glanced around at his surroundings and had a slightly lucid moment. "Why am I lying on the ground?" He tried valiantly to push himself up, but without much success.

I reached down and from a hidden sheath strapped to my lower leg, I pulled out my favorite knife. It was a curved blade, serrated on one side. Topaz jewel slivers encrusted the hilt. They formed a little skull.

The weapon was small enough to rest in the palm of my hand, but when weilded right, could be deadly.

The day's sunlight glinted off of the blade, momentarily blinding me. I smiled at our inebriated friend, then plunged the knife into his leg and sawed a little. I needed spilled blood.

His jeans turned a darker shade of blue as the blood welled up from the wound.

It wasn't enough.

I had to stab him a few more times.

It wasn't until the third puncture the drunk finally registered any pain. He flailed, pitifully. His hands reached out and grasped onto mine. His action covered me in his blood.

Rodolfo snarled as he grabbed the drunk's hands and held pinned them to the dirt road.

I slit our young guests wrists while Rodolfo had them exposed.

A moment transpired while we waited for the blood to flow. Was it possible he was so pickled the blood flow had been suppressed?

But with a little patience, the wounds dribbled a nice sized puddle within the area that had attempted to be my demise the night before.

I stood up, tall, and stretched. Vertebrae popped.

Holding my hands out toward the horizon, my eyes went demon black.

"Egredere!"

Rodolfo continued to hold down the human. He writhed and moaned. The noises were disrupting my summons. Rodolfo looked disgusted as he held the whining mortal. But it didn't take long before the clouds above us coalesced and their underbellies turned dark and brooding. With the sun blocked, shadows lengthened, and from within those dark recesses, a cool wind blew.

That cool breeze turned ice cold, and a low growl rumbled out from the crook of an old elm tree whose branches sprawled out reaching for the sky. In the old days, these stoic remnants had been left at the corners of crossroads to use as property markers for farmyards. Sometimes they even housed something supernatural.

From within the gnarled roots where the shade was deepest, a pair of glowing yellow eyes blinked.

The hellhound hoisted itself from the darkness at the base of the tree. The beast elevated it's snout and sniffed the air. It had been summoned, not sent on a mission. Its behaviour spoke of caution and skepticism.

"Come here boy." I whistled, beckoning it.

The beast crouched and took a few steps towards us, its gaze darting between myself, Rodolfo and the wounded man. Drool hung in long viscous threads from retracted lips. Sharp teeth snapped.

"Come on, I've got a job for you, and a tasty treat."

The dog came forward, slinking low to the ground. These fiends were feral, wild, and violent.

As the mutt closed in, it stretched forward, still drooling, sniffing my extended hand.

It blinked a few times, then visibly relaxed. It stopped snarling and sat on the ground, its tail thumping in short bursts. I assume it had recognized my scent as being superior and higher in rank.

"Now, here's the deal. You get the flesh bag, if you do a little thing for me." I tossed the ripped lapel panel from the dead zombie towards the hellhounds paws. The dog flinched away from the garment. "Catch the witch scent off of this. Whoever animated the corpse had to have left a trace. I want you to track down the bitch who attempted to do away with me. You agree to that, you get him." I pointed to our stabbed, bleeding, and smashed friend. He was currently grasping his leg where I'd sawed him open, and he whined. I hated whining. "Deal?"

The hellhound, dropped its head once.

Deal made.

"Good. Do your thing, find the witch, then come find me."

The dog bent over the piece of fabric, dug its nose into it and pushed the torn fabric around.

I nodded to Rodolfo. He released our captive, stood, and walked over to the car. He opened my door. As I sat into the back of the luxury car my phone started ringing. I turned and looked at the beast, "Good dog." Then I wiped my hands on my pants, dug into my back pocket and pulled out my phone.

I didn't recognize the number. Normally, I wouldn't have answered, but curiosity piqued. I hit the accept button.

"Hello?"

"Hi. Um…" there was hesitancy, but also familiarity. I knew this voice. "Ah, is this Dominic Ronove?"

"It is."

"Oh, hi! It's Malik from the bar. You left in a hurry last night, and I was hoping to…" Malik seemed nervous. "Look, I don't do this very often. Would you be interested in meeting me for coffee?"

My blackened mood lifted, as the dark clouds above us dispersed.

I smiled, remembering Malik. Thinking of his unearthly eyes and cocky self-assuredness, my sour mood almost evaporated despite the fact I could hear teeth on bone and the screams of the man left as the dog's dinner.

"What was that noise? Is everything okay there?"

"Sorry? I don't hear anything. Maybe it's your connection. I think a coffee this afternoon would be a most welcome distraction, Malik.

Maybe even a drink. Where shall I meet you?"

We made plans for later that day, at an outdoor café where we could have a light snack and a well made cappucino, or perhaps one of their signature Ceasars.

As Rodolfo began to pull away from the scene of blood and death at the crossroads, I stared at the hellhound.

If I didn't know any better, I would have sworn it snarled at me. Blood dripped from its muzzle.

As the last of the storm clouds cleared away, the dog dematerialized.

It was hot inside the car. I pushed the button to pull the window down and let the cool summer breezes the hellhound had brought with him waft into the vehicle. The chill relaxed me.

Rodolfo drove down the dirt road, a cloud of dust billowing out behind us.

PART 5

Malik Parsa
Saturday, 12:45pm

I pushed the "end" button on my smartphone, then placed the device on the top of my dresser, right next to a set of carved stone dragons that had been a gift from Scott.

The deed was done.

Just thinking about Dom gave me an adrenaline rush, sending my stomach into twists and turns, and the roiling actions akin to riding a roller coaster. He terrified me and yet the excitement outweighed any danger. I wish I knew why he invoked such a physiological response, but I was captivated with it all.

Taking a couple of steps toward my closet, I opened the doors and picked through the various hangers slung with denim of various colours and levels of distress. I did have a favorite pair. It was a snug fitting faded black jean with fashionable tears in several spots. After several washings, the ripped material had frayed making them appear as if they'd fall off me if yanked the wrong way. Or the right way, depending on who you were.

That brought a smile to my face, and I began to reach for them, but stopped. Would Dom appreciate that kind of look? As much as I knew I should be able to wear whatever the hell was comfortable and exciting for me, I also wanted to make a good impression. And I didn't get the sense bar-wear jeans would excite Dom as much as something a little more refined. And we were meeting at the *Belgravia* which was well-known for being exclusive if not a tad uppity. It had been his suggestion, and I didn't think the high-priced café would appreciate its patrons showing up in slutty bar attire. Despite how much I liked those jeans, Dom struck me as the kind of guy who appreciated the finer things.

His clothes the other night had said, "I'm trying to dress like everyone else.". But the stitching on his boots said custom, and the jeans were top-end designer. Nothing I could ever afford.

Spying at the rest of the clothes in my tiny closet, and pushing several hangers to the side, my pair of khakis I had picked up from the dry-cleaners yesterday during my lunch break spoke to me. The thin plastic bag still wrapped around them seemed strangulating and yet, the exact thing I was looking for.

I pulled them out of the closet and ripped the protective layer away. A waft of chemical cleaner assaulted me briefly, and then dispersed as quickly as it appeared. With a beige pair of pants, I needed a shirt that was going to spice the date up a little, but still maintain the look I was going for; well-dressed, capable adult who is responsible yet fun. Did I even own such a shirt?

"Well?" From the doorway to my bedroom, Scott and Amber had crowded in and were now both giving me the stink eye. "What happened? Are you going to meet up?" Amber was more excited about this than I was.

Okay, that was maybe a little lie.

After last night's food foray, Amber had disclosed her apartment was clear on the other side of the city, and she didn't drive. A cab home would have cost her a fortune, so Scott offered his bed, and a ride the next morning. Scott had slept on the couch, and then after breakfast, and more chatting, Amber was still here. Not that *that* was a bad thing. I was growing rather fond of her.

"Are you going out on a date with him?" Scott's voice sounded upbeat and inquisitive and hopeful. The expression on his face however, told a different tale.

At this point, Scott's reaction to Dom had me ruffled. Scott and I weren't committed to each other in any way, shape or form. I didn't understand his obvious distaste for the man I had just met. As soon as Amber was out of our hair, I'd be having words with him.

"Yeah, we are. This afternoon at the *Belgravia*. I'm going to meet him there at 1:30. A mid-afternoon lunch. Hopefully, if I play my cards right, that will lead to late afternoon cocktails, then dinner, then a sleepover."

"Damn, you got yourself a plan. Ugh, I'm so jealous. I've been wanting to go to that café *forever!*" Amber put her hands on her hips and pursed her lips. "I'm impressed."

"Just be careful. If you need me to come pick you up, text me."

I squinted at Scott. From Amber's perspective, his choice of words would have sounded like a good roommate's buddy system. We'd never had such an arrangement. I ignored the bizarre response.

"I have no idea what shirt to wear with this." I said feeling flummoxed and throwing my hands up in the air.

"You're wearing work pants?" Scott sneered.

"Dude, what gives?" Any chance of ignoring him flew out the window.

"What do you mean?" Scott shrugged. "I've never seen you wear those pants other than to go to work, so is this a business meeting, or a date?"

I glared at Scott. "It's supposed to be a date, but I don't get the impression he's the kind of guy whose going to like me in faded torn jeans. I'm trying to make a good first impression. Not show up in stained and worn-out sweats." I pointed to Scott's current pant predicament. "Besides, it's the *Belgravia*."

"Hey, don't knock grey sweats on a guy." Amber raised her eyebrows and smiled.

"You need to get laid." I said to our newest house guest.

"God, no shit." Amber invited herself into my bedroom, walked over to my closet, and peered into it. The doors were still wide open. She riffled through my shirts.

"No, no....definitely no." She turned her head to look at my pants which I had lain on the bed. "Hmm…" She continued flipping through my wardrobe. While she was preoccupied, I gave Scott a dirty look.

He returned it.

Yup, something was definitely up.

"This. This shirt is perfect!" Amber turned and thrust the garment towards me.

"Oh dear god, really? Tracey gave that to me last Christmas. I have never worn it."

Tracey was my last foster mother before I had finally moved out on my own. She had been the most decent and caring out of all the homes I had been through and had tried to give me and my foster brothers some semblance of stability. Her husband was a real shit though and the only reason he had agreed to foster kids in his house were the monthly government checks that rolled in. I liked Tracey, despite the fact she tried too hard. She had been an awkward parental figure at a time in my life when I was ready to leave parents behind.

To this day she kept in touch and every Christmas she sent a gift.

The shirt was a deep forest green with a dense maroon paisley print on it. The paisley was just a tad over the top for me.

"Why haven't you worn this? This is gorgeous, and it matches your pants perfectly."

"It kinda does." Scott offered from the doorway.

I sneered at him. We were so having words later.

Striding out into the living room, where Scott and Amber were currently reclining on the sofa, I stood in the middle of the living room and did a slow twirl.

"And?"

"Wow. You clean up great! But then, I already knew that. Everyone knew that the minute you walked into the bar last night." Amber was almost drooling.

"You know, Scott is sitting right beside you and he's better looking than I am." Scott was still on my shit list, but I needed to divert all the attention I was getting. The date thing was now making me really uncomfortable and horrifyingly nervous and thrusting me into far too much of a spotlight. The look in Amber's eyes as she gawked at me was nothing short of lascivious.

"True, but you're shining now, baby. If Scott had gotten all shaved and showered and dressed up, I'd be all goo-goo eyed over him. Right now, it's all about you."

"Scott, don't you have to drive Amber home?"

They looked at each other and laughed.

It was at that moment I hated them both just a little and realized that Amber had just become our new bestie.

I could live with that.

PART 6

Dominic Ronove
Saturday, 1:30pm

"Well, hello there." I said to myself as I studied Malik walking toward my table wearing a tight-around-the-chest, button up, paisley-print shirt and a pair of khakis. His chest muscles stretched the fabric. The outdoor patio turned out to be a rather popular spot. I had to bribe the hostess in order to select a table that provided at least some privacy, yet still allowed us to watch the comings and goings within the restaurant.

Malik beamed at me. I could smell his nervousness, like sticky, dripping tar.

I stood up to welcome him. I might be a demon, but I have manners.

There was an awkward *"now what"* moment. Do I shake his hand? Lean in for a kiss on the cheek? Humans.

Malik decided to go in for the hug, however brief. I reciprocated, giving the compulsory pat on the shoulder while we embraced, doing the "bro" hug version, but I flinched as Malik got dangerously close to my concealed shoulder wound. Despite my awkward movement, I took the opportunity to smell him. Humans are vile creatures, but every now and then one comes along who is rather delicious. Malik was the latter.

He reminded me of a nighttime, rocket-ride on a motorcycle. Worn leather, metal, night breezes and engine oil. I could honestly say I had never encountered anyone who had such a distinct scent. Malik, it would seem, was a veritable delight of uniqueness.

I released him, and we sat down.

"You've been here before?" Malik glanced around the patio. The large planter boxes were stuffed to capacity with annual flowers, surrounding our table with a jungle of well tended plants. Their garish display assaulted the eyes with a riot of pinks, purples, reds, and white.

"A few times, yes." Just as I finished our server appeared.

"Dom," Chelsea cooed. "It's lovely to see you again."

The unmistakable odor of burnt black pepper wafted off of her.

Mental note – this one was ready.

"Chelsea," I smiled. "It's been a while."

"It sure has, handsome." She took the capped end of her pen and playfully poked my shoulder. Thankfully, she hadn't poked the side where Rodolfo had extracted a tree branch. From the size of Malik's opened eyes, this tete-a-tete with our server would be begging questions as soon as she left. "You boys want something to drink?"

"You know what I really want?" I cocked an eyebrow at Chelsea.

"Do tell."

"One of those house Ceasars. But a double, and extra spicy. Malik, care to join me?"

"Ah, sure. That sounds good."

Chelsea nodded and then strutted away. She glanced over her

shoulder toward me and gave a look that could only be described as lude. She was heading down all the wrong paths in life. I could tell I had another contract to be signed in the not-to-distant future.

"So, she a past date?"

"Who, Chelsea?" I scoffed. "She would like that, but no."

Malik shifted in his seat and busied himself with one of the menus Chelsea had dropped on the table.

"Okay, you have questions. Out with them."

"Well, it's not really any of my business. I mean, we're just trying to see if we're compatible? Interested in each other? Right? I have a hundred questions, but—"

"No, it's okay Malik. Ask away. I tell you whatever you want to know." Glancing at Malik, I attempted to give him one of those magically convincing stares that would covey warmth, trust, and sincerity. I had an arsenal of looks I'd mastered over the years. They all had their uses, and came in handy. Remember, gaining a human's trust was paramount to my job.

"Seriously?"

"Yes. Ask away."

"Okay. Gay, Bi, Pan? What's the deal?"

"Does it matter?"

"It shouldn't, but I've never dated anyone who was anything but gay. Just something to have to mentally tackle, I suppose." Malik gave me a half smile. For a guy who looked as good as he did, and who seemed to have an overabundance of confidence, I was surprised at his answer. My sexual preferences aside, there were a ton of mental gymnastics he would have to do if he knew the truth about me.

"Well, I'm not sure what kind of label to use, to be honest. When I find someone I'm interested in, I either go into business with them, or fuck them." It wasn't a lie, but it was a test. I wanted to see how he'd respond.

"Cool. Okay. And so, you'd either open a restaurant with me or fuck me. I can live with at least those two options for now."

I laughed out loud. He lifted his menu up, pretending to study it, which hid half his face.

"So, Dom, huh?"

"Yeah. Why?"

"I don't know. Not sure I like that name for you. I mean, I get it. It's your name short, quick, and easy to say, but I can't help thinking of some kinky dungeon mistress, and even though you are about as mysterious, and I get the sense that there's even a bit of a kinky streak in you, I don't think I can call you Dom."

I grinned and nodded. "What would you like to call me?"

"At minimum, I'd like to call you for a second date." He glanced over the top of the menu he was holding. I could tell by the way his eyes were partially squinted that he had amused himself and there was a huge smile behind the laminated sheet he held obscuring his devilishly handsome face. He put the menu down on his plate. He was smiling. Ear to ear. "How about just Dominic?"

"That'll be fine."

The Ceasars arrived plugged full of goodies. I liked them this way. A spicy peperoni stick, a celery stalk, a pickled bean, and a vibrant pink shrimp precariously dangling on the seasoned rim of the glass left no room to sip the cocktail, but I managed it anyway. The salt and pepper edge coupled nicely with the clamato juice as the spices heated everything up.

Malik had fished out most of his accoutrement, placed them on his side plate, and had taken a healthy swallow of his drink. His cheeks flushed as the spice level registered.

"Holy hell, that is hot." Malik sucked in air through puckered lips, then went for his water glass.

We ordered food, chatted in short bursts, and my assumptions about Malik were spot on. Young, slightly nieve, energetic, ambitious but not overtly career-focused. But every now and then he'd say something that surprised me. He was all gusto, but was afraid of heights. He's overly comfortable with his sexuality, yet wasn't all that experienced. All the while he was talking, and I kept him talking about himself as much as possible, I took in his ease, his comfort, his good looks, willingness to tell me everything, and those unearthly topaz eyes.

Humans generally feel ill at ease around me. Most are decidedly uncomfortable in my presence, even if they don't know why. Occasionally the Ambers and Chelseas of the world find that innate sense of danger a turn on, and my interactions with those people quickly escalate into lascivious behaviour. It's a rare oddity if someone can spot what I really am. It has happened, but only a handful of times. But this lunch with Malik verged on a once in a lifetime event. After reflecting back through my years, I couldn't say anyone sat and ate with me, bantering about their life with such naturalness.

And yet, here I was, with Malik doing exactly that.

"What about you? What do you do for work?" I had become lost in my own thoughts losing control of the conversation. Malik had snatched that away from me and now turned the tables.

Dammit.

"Ah, well, I deal in transactions." I couldn't have been more vague if I tried.

"Like, what? A financial broker? You're one of those investment bankers?"

"A broker, yes you could say that. Definitely in investments. I specialize in getting people what they want. For a price." That was about all I was prepared to say.

"Sounds fascinating when you put it like that. Even though I program code all day long, math and numbers still evade me. Couldn't balance my bank statement if I tried. I'm sincerely impressed with those who can wrangle numbers and make them make sense. Coding is all patterns, and then repeating the patterns that work. There's even a bit of creativity to it. I like those parts." Malik shrugged as he speared a chunk of his tukey queso enchilada with his fork.

"Well, its not just about numbers. A good portion of my job is keeping my bosses happy. My work keeps me busy, and I work odd hours. It's not often I get a lot of spare time to do things like this."

"Well, then, I feel fortunate that I've managed to monopolize some of that time." Malik said with half-lidded eyes and uneven grin, which made me feel...

Made me feel content? Happy? What the hell was this?

It had been a century, or longer, since I had noted these sensations. My well-worn flesh suit had had years of training, and adjusting to my energy. I had thought such complicated and messy emotions had been banished.

It took a moment of calmness before the emotion subsided. I wasn't sure I liked it.

It wasn't unpleasant, but...

What was it about this guy?

"It's such a beautiful day." I said, attempting to change the subject and distract me from my own thoughts. "Tell me, if we weren't doing this, wouldn't you be hanging out with your friends? You seemed to have quite the gang with you last night." As much as I didn't want any unruly mental jumping-jacks, I certainly wasn't going to walk away from this situation. Malik intrigued me.

I had to know more about him.

"The guys? There a good bunch, but, you know, they're all friends. And friends aren't going to get you laid." After he said it, Malik turned beat red. "Not that I'm insinuating—"

I held my hand up while I chuckled to myself, "It's quite all right. I get it." Images flashed in my mind of a naked Malik bent over the edge of my bed as I nailed him from behind. And as if on queue, sensing my sudden keener interest in continuing my discussion with Malik, a black mastiff came trotting towards me.

For fuck's sake, not now.

The dog lept easily, and gracefully over the planter boxes. The flowers still intact after the beastly animal cleared the jump. It padded itself over to my side and glared at me. I put my head in my hands and rubbed my face.

No rest for the wicked.

"Ah, wow, that's a big dog who really seems to like you." Malik had pushed his seat away from the table placing some distance between himself and the gargantuan beast.

"I can't believe this." I shook my head. "I'm so sorry." I had to come up with a plausible lie. I couldn't very well tell Malik I'd sacrificed a drunk this morning, raised a hellhound from the pit and sent it off in search of a trio of sibling witches who had attempted to kill me. "Ah... this, this is my dog. His name is Cerberus." I made a stupid lopsided grin. I mean, technically the hellhound was Cerberus, they all were. I glared at the animal.

"Like the three headed houd of hell?" Malik asked.

Well, shock me with jumper cables. "The one and same." I squinted at Malik and nodded in acknowledgement. "And it would seem today he's a bit of an escape artist."

"Do you live around here?"

"No. Nowhere near here."

"That's amazing. He got out and followed your scent! Wow! Good boy."

Cerberus's tail wagged and thumped on the concrete patio stones. Its massive muzzle swung over toward Malik. My entire body tensed. I had to give credit to the fiend. It had been efficient about its task and had done exactly as commanded. Obviously he had located the witches and then set out to find me.

Thank the ninth level that the mutt also had enough brains to conceal its true appearance. But I wasn't confident Malik's presence wouldn't spark some primal instinct to tear apart my date and run off with his soul.

Malik leaned over and pat his leg, "Come here, boy."

"Ah, Malik, I don't know how friendly—" The hound sniffed the air in Malik's direction, then took two steps over and repositioned himself beside my lunchtime companion and placed his drooling snout in Malik's lap.

Malik reached down and stroked the charcoal fur on the top of the beasts head. It's tail wagged back and forth.

Well, I'll be damned.

"Mastiff, right? I don't think I've ever seen a black one before. He's adorable. Funny, you don't strike me as the type to own a pet." Malik continued to pet the beast, and even had his hand under the hound's mouth.

I almost couldn't watch.

"Yes, well, surprise!" I said, trying my damndest to keep tabs on the hellhound. I had never seen one sidle up to a human.

Malik was all kinds of unusual.

Just then Chelsea appeared looking extremely flustered. Behind her, the establishment's manager stood in the doorway to the main part of the restaurant with his arms crossed looking very perturbed. "I'm sorry, Dom, but Gustov is about to lose his mind. You cannot have your dog here. It's against health code regulations."

"Yes, well, he wasn't supposed to leave the house either. Apologies. I'll remove him." I turned to look at Malik. "I'm sorry. I'm going to have to cut this short and take him home, and then have words with my staff on keeping him secure."

"Aw, that's too bad. Why don't we get the rest of the food to go and take him for a walk?"

"Well, I don't have a lead with me, and as you can see, he doesn't have his collar on."

"Oh, right, I guess!" Malik glanced down to look at the dog's thick neck.

Putting a collar on a hellhound would *never* happen.

"And to be honest, I've never seen him interact well with other people. This," I waved my finger at Malik's lap where the dog still rested his head, "is highly unusual. I generally only take him for very late night walks. Less people. Certainly less other dogs."

"Oh, I don't believe a word. Look at him! He's such a good puppy." Malik grabbed both sides of the dogs head and shoved his face right up to the beast's maw. "Who's a good puppy? You are. Such a good dog." Malik leaned in a kissed the dog's forehead.

"Okay, well I think I should return Cerberus." I stood, placing my napkin over my half eaten meal. Getting Malik away from the hellhound seemed far more pressing than removing the dog from the restaurant's patio. I pulled my wallet out and fished out a few bills and left them on the table. There was more than enough money to cover our entire bill, and leave a hefty tip for Chelsea. Hopefully she'd enjoy it before I signed her burnt, black peppery scented soul away for food.

"Awww…okay, I understand. You don't have to pay for my meal!" Malik's eyes went wide as he saw the amount of money I left on the table.

"It's no problem."

"Transactions pay well." Malik ogled the couple of hundreds I'd left.

"That they do." I grinned. If he only knew the half of it.

"Um, well, do you want to get together later? Maybe we can go for a drink?"

"I'd like that, but tonight's not good." I glanced down at the dog. As soon as we left, I knew he'd take me to the where he'd located the witches. I would have business to take care of. "But I'll give you a call as soon as I can. I would like to see you again. Hopefully our interruption—" I glanced down at the hellhound, "hasn't ruined things. You're an intriguing person, Malik."

Malik grinned, giving me a come hither look, "I'll take that as a compliment. And Cerberus couldn't ruin anything."

The beast returned its attention to Malik, its tail wagging affectionately. Snapping my fingers, I reoriented Cereberus's gaze back in my direction. "I really do apologize," The hell-beast glared at me. "Let's go." I commanded. The dog pulled himself away from Malik. "Later, Malik. I look forward to our next *date*." This had been a date, hadn't it, as short as it had been. We'd gotten to know a little bit about each other. He continued to fascinate me.

"I like the sound of that." The hell hound turned and looked back at Malik, his tail wagging. He let out a little whine.

"I've never seen him take to someone else like this."

"Maybe that's a good sign." Malik offered as he reached out to pet the beast's rump.

"Perhaps." I said, nodded once, then turned and escorted the mutt out of the restaurant and away from Malik.

PART 7

Dominic Ronove
Saturday, 3:57pm

As soon as we were a few blocks away from the restuaruant, walking down an older street graced on each side with massive trees lining the boulevard, I glanced down at the dog, "What the hell were you thinking? You could have waited for me to leave."

As we passed under a spot with a particularly dense canopy where the shadows grew long and the tree trunks were thick, the dog morphed in a heartbeat into a tall thin man wearing all black.

"Waiting for you to be done eating food, or leaving the establishment you were at wasn't part of our deal. Your intructions were perfectly clear. Scent the zombie back to the witches who animated it, then fetch you and show you where the sorceresses live. I followed that to the letter in exchange for the morsel of food you left me. By the way, next time, something a little less toxic would be appreciated."

"Excuse me?" I halted and glared at the man. A shank of blond hair fell into his eyes.

"I couldn't even eat all of it the flesh was so polluted."

"Oh, that must have been terrible for you." I continued to stroll ahead. The hound kept pace, but sneered at me. The beast was verging on insubordination.

"All right, look. I came when you summoned me. I took the expected offering. You'd have done no less if you were summoned to a crossroads. There are rules."

"Yes, be that as it may, but there is a hierarchy, an order—"

"Yes, one that is about to be turned on its head."

I stopped in my tracks, again, and stared at him. "What do you mean?"

Cerberus paused, turned and studied me, then twisted and kept walking towards the location of the witches domicile he had scouted.

"I don't know yet, exactly. But something is going on. Someone somewhere is trying to upset the apple cart." He pointed toward the ground, telling me that the rank and file of the demon world was once again shifting. It was a cyclical thing really. No demon is ever happy where they land. We're always trying to improve our situation. Even demons are tortured at some level. The higher up the food chain you are, the better off you are.

"That's not really news."

"This situation is." He continued walking, but was silent.

"Are you baiting me?"

"Well, if you're not interested." He shrugged, then turned his head to glance at me. "How certain are you of your position?"

"Rather."

"Hmm. As am I."

"Alright, out with it. What do you know?"

"Well, see that comes at a price. And truly, I don't know much, but enough."

"Enough with vague allusions to grand plots to overthrow me. What's going on?"

"I want something in return." Cereberus stopped walking, turned and faced me. Bold move.

"What do you want?"

"To be yours."

"Excuse me?" I have had some odd requests in my time, but having a hellhound willingly offer themselves up to me? This was a first. The species was notoriously feral.

"I want your protection. Plain and simple. I want something better than what I've got. You can offer that to me. I heard what you said to the boy."

"He's not a boy."

"He's a human in his twenties. We're both several hundred years old. He's a boy."

"You're attitudinal."

"And?"

"Seven hells. Are you always such a pain in the ass?"

"Probably. I'm good at what I do, but dogs don't exactly get much for street cred. We're treated like shit, down in the basement, so I'd rather be a lap dog up top." Cerberus cocked an eyebrow while glaring at me.

"You're a little big to be a lap dog. And I sure as hell don't need you shedding all over the place or trying to sleep in my bed at night."

"Really? I hear you'll sleep with anything."

"Do you want me to put you down right here?"

"Then you wouldn't find those witches, would you?"

I rolled my eyes. This thing was trying my patience. "What exactly do I get out of this arrangement you propose? You want my protection. Protection from whom? Or what?"

"If you mark me, then no other can summon me. If I'm yours, then I do your bidding and yours alone. Call me a constant companion if you will. I can be some muscle in difficult situations. Call for me and I show up, or I'll just pad behind you where ever you go. Your choice, really. Plus there aren't many creatures who can sniff out residual magic quite like I can. And I can slip into the under realm and retrieve info. I hear you don't like making return trips home. Haven't been back to see Daddy in a long time."

"Yes, well, Lucifer and I have an 'arrangement.'"

"One that has an expiration date?"

"Eventually. Nothing I'm concerned about currently."

"But if you were breaking the rules of that deal, and word got back to the big guy, then…" Cereberus continued his cocky look.

"And who would be telling him of such lies?"

"But are they lies? Elisha and Rodolfo are far past their original contract dates, are they not?"

"Yes, but they are useful."

"They're also human. I hear bending and breaking contracts is forbidden. And going on dates with humans? Think the old man would like that?"

I glared at him.

"So who is stirring up shit? Who would be so brazen to come after me?"

"Probably the same demon who gave the witches I scouted out for you, the tome necessary to summon you."

"Really?" Okay, that caught my attention.

"I can smell another one of your rank in the mix. But I don't know

66

who. Not yet."

"Alright. That just solidifed your offer." The tall man smiled, crooked and toothy. He was actually a strapping wiry man, and not hard to look at it either. He did have a rather nasty scar across one side of his face. Something I hadn't noticed while he was in beast mode. But healed scars only meant he knew how to handle himself in a dangerous fight, and had survived to tell the tale. "I'll make you mine. You'll be my new housedog. You will take all my finalized contracts to their destination and figure out which other demon is plotting my demise. Yes?"

"Yes"

"And I should call you what exactly? Cerberus in dog form, especially when Malik's around, otherwise there will be questions. But when you're mimicking a human?"

"I don't really care. Call me what you like. Until twenty minutes ago I had no name."

I squinted, discerning a namesake. "How about Miles? It's Latin roots mean 'soldier'. That's what you'll be for me."

"So be it."

"Don't make me regret this." I added.

"You won't."

"All right, if you want my mark, then..." I pointed at his chest.

Miles unbuttoned his shirt, peeled it away and exposed his chest to me. His body was taught. There wasn't an ounce of fat on him, which meant he wasn't getting fed enough. There were a myriad of white scar lines across his flesh. You didn't live for as long as he had at the bottom of the chain of command without wracking up a toll. His body hair wasn't particularly thick, which surprised me. I would have thought being a dog, he'd be more hirsuite. But there was enough fur on his chest and torso to obscure the worst of his battle marks.

67

I placed my hand on the center of his chest. I had to wriggle my fingers to get through his hair so that I had good contact with the skin.

"*Hoc est corpus meum.*" From under my fingers a blinding flash of light.

Miles, grimmaced.

"You'll live."

"You didn't say it would hurt."

"I just carved my mark on your rib bone. How was that not going to hurt?"

"Demons." Miles snarled and shook his head. He buttoned up his shirt. The deal was done. He was mine. Permanently. The only way to remove my sigil would be to scrape it off.

As we continued our walk, he shifted back to his natural form, and Cerberus led the way. Seemed as if I'd gained a pet.

Well, that would make Malik happy.

We stopped several houses away, just to be sure no witchy senses came into play ruining our upper hand. I needed the element of surprise. If these witches had enough power to corral me into a snare, even with a book of spells, then I'd have to keep my distance until I was ready to strike.

Besides, a tall, dark, imposing man with a large black dog glaring at you from across the street would raise anyone's hackles, never mind witches.

A brunette with thick, long hair tied up in a pony was out in the yard with a shovel, digging away in the garden. I crouched where I could

hide myself behind some shubbery. Not exactly upper-rank demon behaviour – but you do what you have to do to get the job done. Cerberus
thumped down beside me and lay his head in the grass. Apparently he
was done his job.

As I watched her work away at some gnarled root system, two
young men came out of the house. One, the same hair colour as the girl
in the garden, the other was blond. Despite the slight variation on the
hair colour, it was very obvious all three were siblings.

"Why are you working so hard on that? All you had to do was ask."
The man with the blond hair lifted his hand in the air and twisted his
palm while his fingers danced through the air.

The roots that had been so deeply burried into the soil came alive,
writhing and squirming. I have to admit, it was fascinating to watch the
remnants of a dead plant come back to life and lift itself out of the dirt.
As soon as the mangled roots were out of the hole, the man stopped his
finger motions and the skeletal ball of roots fell motionless at the girl's
feet.

"For fuck's sake Noah!" The girl glanced around. I ducked down
further. "What the hell are you thinking?"

"Oh my god, relax Riley, no one is out."

"That's not the point."

"Grayson, let's go."

The two got in what you would refer to as a 'reliable automobile',
cranked the engine, reversed down the driveway, and then drove off in
the opposite direction from where I had been hiding.

This was perfect timing. She was all alone. And I already knew
that she was the most powerful out of the three, so singling her out and
getting her dealt with first would make the other two that much easier.

Movement out of the corner of my eye caught my attention. Swinging my head in the direction from where we had come, a little old lady with one of those roller carts was making her way up the street. But she had spotted me and the dog, quite obviously hiding, and spying on the girl.

I leered at her. I didn't need any interuptions.

As I continued my gaze toward her she became visibly upset. Her look morphed from one of surprise, to one of fear. This was about to get out of control.

And then I had an idea.

"All right, puppy. Time to go to work. I need you to watch me. Understand? No one comes near me." The dog canted his head to one side. He clearly didn't know what I was about to do, but he'd figure it out pretty quick.

It's not something I do often, as the meat sack I've grown fond of can react badly from my presence being missing. Decay is a problem once the demon energy has left, and this body was old. Actually, old enough for me to have consider getting a new one, but I had grown accustomed to my human height, muscles, and stoic furtive features. And changing bodies presented difficulties I'd rather not have to deal with. So I protected my meat suit, despite my recent recklessness.

As I wrenched my demon self out of my sock puppet, it tumbled lifeless to the ground. Cerberus looked momentarily confused, and then saw me, in my demonic energy form, and he understood. Carefully grabbing me by the neck, he hauled me over so I lay tight next to the bushes we had used as a blind.

Some folks would never see me while in this shape. For those who do, they interpret the visual differently. Most see a shadow, and get an ill-at-ease feeling from it. Others percieve a ghost like apparation, but I'm far darker. Most ghosts are luminescent to some degree. I am like the ink toner from a printer cartridge which fell out and coalesced into a shape.

It's the rare humans who have some true psychic ability that will see a tall thin stretched shadow man.

Grandma didn't know I was coming. She had turned around and was scuttling back the way she had come, her two wheeler roller cart squeaking as she tried to go as fast as she could.

It wasn't nearly fast enough.

As I reached out and grabbed the back of her shoulder, I effortlessly plunged myself into her worn out, saggy, and floppy body. Correction. The skin was floppy, from years of use. Her bones were stiff and brittle. I could have easily ended her life by snapping her neck just by thinking about it. But I needed her.

As my melding completed, I halted her actions, closed her eyes, and let my energies flow into her brain, finding the pathways that connected her thoughts to her soul, and ruptured the thin blood vessels that pebbled her body like lesions on a leper. Within a heartbeat, an arythmic, unstable heartbeat, she was mine.

Turning around, I continued the walk down the street until I was across the street from the solitary witch, still digging in her garden. Then I continued until I was standing in her driveway. I was so close to her. This witch who had attempted to harness me and send me back to hell, or worse, end my existence was in mortal danger and she had no idea. Some witch. So close. I could smell the sweat on her body, and the cheap perfumed deodorant that she wore everyday. I licked my lips.

"Dear, I'm so sorry to bother you. But I suddenly feel very hot. I wonder if you could grab me a glass of water?"

She turned around.

"Oh, hi Mrs. Winterfield. What are you – where's Birney? Doesn't

71

he usually take you shopping on Saturdays?"

"Oh, honey, yes," I searched the inside of Mrs. Winterfield's rather scattered brain. Honestly she didn't have much time left. Everything about this body was tired. And then I saw it. Birney, her husband of forty-six years was still in bed from last night. She didn't want to disturb him. Poor dumb thing. She didn't realize Birney was dead. "Birney, had a rough night last night. I'm letting him sleep in. You know how it gets when you get to be this old, dear."

Riley glanced at her watch, noted the time and raised an eyebrow.

"Sweetie, some water?" I reminded her.

"Oh, yes, of course. Come here." Riley walked down the driveway, slipped her hand into the crook of my elbow and carefully navigated us both up the front porch. I really played it up. I could have ran this body anywhere and beat the hell out of Riley, but this was a game. A game of trust. And right now, I was winning.

She escorted me through her front door, and then took me into the formal living room. Something few folks had anymore, but this house was an old victorian, built in the early 1900's. The room on the front of the house had big bright windows allowing sunshine to dance in from the outside making the tiny room cheery and pleasant. The finishings within the house were detailed and well-crafted, but that spoke to the era it had been built. This neighborhood was just west of the downtown core, where Malik and I had only earlier been enjoying our lunch. This tight residential area only comprised a few blocks, but Glenora was famously known for it's wealthy families and decadent historical houses.

I sat on an antique curved back sofa, upholstered in plush and silky caramel velvet.

"You just sit here. I'll go get you some water, okay?"

There was a look of concern and perhaps worry in Riley's eyes. She wasn't buying some small part of this. Either she had figured me out, or there was some alarm over Mrs. Winterfield, I couldn't tell which. But the gig was almost up. I had to act fast.

As soon as Riley exited the room and disappeared down the hallway, I got up, and ran out the front door as fast as the two knobby, damn near crippled legs would carry me, found the shovel from the front yard's gardening task, and then waltzed back into the house, following the path Riley had taken, until I heard the tap running.

I entered into the kitchen as silently as possible and raised the shovel. Riley pulled the cold water leaver to the side to stop the flow of water. As she turned with a glass full for Mrs. Winterfield, I slammed the shovel against the side of her head.

Blood sprayed across the kitchen. Riley's eyes fluttered, then rolled. Her knees gave out. The glass dropped from her hand and shattered on the floor.

Riley crumpled like a marionette with cut strings into a heap on the floor.

I threw the shovel to the side of the room, clanking and banging various objects before it came to rest. I walked over to the comatose witch and kicked her to make sure she was good and out.

At that moment, Cerberus appeared behind me then morphed into Miles.

"Smooth."

"You are supposed to be watching my body." Mr's Winterfield's face scrowled at the dog.

"I figured you might need some help. Looks like I was right."

I was about to argue with his train of logic, but Mrs. Winterfield's frail body couldn't contain my energy any longer. I sensed a rupture.

"This body is disgusting. Wait here."

As I ripped myself out of Mrs. Winterfield, I felt several more blood vessels *snap* as I left her. Looks like the old bag would be joining her late husband.

PART 8

Malik Parsa
Saturday, 4:15pm

Disappointment gnawed at my insides. This hadn't gone to plan, and the fact that my date had ended so abruptly left me with a rather snarly temperment. I was supposed to be still spending time with my dark and dreamy suitor, extending our afternoon into cocktails, dinner and then a sleepover.

Granted, shit happens, but what were the chances that his dog would escape and then track his owner down?

But what a dog.

So cute!

Turning to go down the hall to my bedroom, I walked right into Scott. My hands went out to steady both of us, and I ended up with fistfulls of chest hair and muscle.

"Sorry, dude." I sighed, backed away and turned into my bedroom. I knew I had to have a conversation with him on why he disapproved of me going out on a date, but I wasn't in the mood.

"What happened?"

My shoulders slumped as I frowned. "Is it that obvious?"

"For a guy who's pretty chipper most of the time, yeah. Was he an asshole? He looks like an asshole." Scott, decked out in tight fitting shorts, a beige pair that really showed off his, *ahem*, attributes, leaned against the door jam. He didn't have any other clothes on, which was typical.

I had to admit, he was really good looking. There were abs everywhere.

"No, he wasn't an asshole at all. He was a perfect gentleman and a super nice guy. But the weirdest thing happened."

"Okay, tell me all about it."

I started to strip. I was done looking all nice and the dressy clothes did nothing but reinforce how disheartened I found myself.

"Well, we had a great lunch, and by the way if we can ever afford to we have to go there. The food was amazeballs. But man, expensive!" I pulled my shirt off, walked over to the closet and hung it up. "We were about half way through lunch when this massive dog jumped over the planters and trotted right over to our table. It was his dog!"

"What, like he left it tied up outside the restaurant and the thing got loose?" Scott had a thing with pet owners leaving their dogs strung up outside stores.

"No, that's the weird part." I undid my belt buckle. Scott and I were perfectly comfortable being naked around each other, so I wasn't going to stop. Besides, I needed comfy clothes. I took my pants and hung them up. I looked after my clothes, not like my roommate, who I guaranteed you had a pile of clean clothes lumped over the chair in his bedroom, and possibly a rank and nasty heap of items that needed immediate washing socked away in his closet. "He had left his dog at home, which was no where near the restaurant. Apparently the dog got out. Sweetest beast ever. But big. Damn. Really big." I yanked off my underwear and socks, pitched them into my clothes hamper and then went to my dresser drawer to retrieve my 'around-the-house-lazy-clothes'.

"And that was bad, because?" Scott moved into my bedroom and sat on the end of my bed.

Pulling out my sweats, I sat on the bed next to Scott and started to pull them on. "Nothing bad about it, but the server came out to our table, all flustered, and said Dom couldn't have his dog on the patio. I mean, obviously, it's a restaurant, but that pretty much called off the rest of our date. I suggested a walk in the park with the pooch, but Dominic didn't have a lead or leash. So then I thought maybe we could get together later."

"Wow, you pulled out all the stops. He didn't bite?"

"I wish he had bitten me – Dominic – not the dog." I glanced at Scott to see if he caught my drift. He had. He smiled. But it was one of those grins that people made when they were sympathizing with you and trying to make everything better. I rolled my eyes and continued without trying to make any further funny remarks. "No, he wanted to, but he has to work tonight. So he said he would call me. Kinda sounded a little like a blow off."

"Ah, but not a blow job."

"No. dammit all. That would have been nice."

Scott raised an eyebrow. "Well, you know…" He licked his lips.

"Really? We haven't done that in…what, like almost a year."

"Yeah, so? I haven't had any fun with anyone in a long time, and you're feeling miserable. I can't think of a better way to cheer someone up." Scott placed a warm hand on my thigh.

77

My dick started to thicken which was really obvious in sweatpants. As much as I really wished to be doing this exact thing with Dominic, that scenario wasn't going to happen. At least not tonight, and who knew if it ever would. On Dominic's own admittance, he didn't get a lot of free time. Sounded like he was married to his job.

I shrugged, partly to myself, giving up hope of making some kind of connection with Dominic, and partly in agreeance with Scott's sexual proposition.

"That's not where my dick is." I said.

"Oh, I see." Scott moved his hand over my lengthening and hardening cock. "I think I found it."

"Yup. That's it."

"Didn't take long for you to get hard." Scott shifted his hand and slipped it under the material, his fingers crawling through my public hair and then gliding over my rod.

"I think you walked in here hard. Those shorts, dude." I slid over on the bed so I was snuggled right up against Scott. I placed my palm over the rather obscene bulge in his shorts. Scott was good looking. Furry, too, which I loved. But he also had a huge dick, which I loved even more. It really was a shame we didn't match emotionally.

"Okay, so, this is happening?" Scott squeezed my rock hard boner. I felt a small pearl of pre-cum leak out.

"What the fuck, why not."

Scott laughed, "Don't sound so enthusiastic." He stood up, and turned to face me. "You want to do the honours?"

"Ah, yeah, you know that's one of my favorite parts."

"It's all yours." One side of Scott's mouth twerked up in a lopsided grin.

I guess conversations with Scott over his dislike of Dominic would have to wait. I reached up to Scott's obscenely tight shorts, popped the button and then slowly slid the zipper down.

Scott's excited cock fell into my waiting hands. A part of me wondered how the zipper ever held back such a monster.

We ordered pizza.

We drank wine.

We watched some horrible zombie flick from a streaming service we couldn't believe we gave money to every month, but somehow never remembered to unsubscribe from. We also cuddled under a massive blanket with Amber sitting in between the two of us. She hid her face in either Scott's shoulder or mine during every jump scare the movie offered.

I was right, Amber had become our new bestie. Guaranteed that at this late hour, she would be spending the night, which meant either one of two things. Scott would be sleeping on the couch, because he was just too much of a gentleman to make her do it, or, Scott would be sleeping in my bed. Given our afternoon frolic, I was placing bets on the latter.

"Okay, that movie was awful. I will definitely be having nightmares tonight." Amber leaned forward and grabbed her Cosmo from the coffee table. She had brought one of those preprepared mix drinks in a two litre bottle. I didn't even know they came in such containers.

I equated it to box wine.

Amber turned to me. "So, how was the date? You haven't mentioned it, and neither have you." She swung her head around to face Scott.

Neither of us said anything.

"Oh, all right. It's going to be like that. So, let me think." She pursed her lips and then gave both of us a side glance, sizing us up. "It's one of two scenarios. Nope. Three."

"What are you talking about?" I shifted my weight so my back was resting against the couch's arm so that I could at least see their faces.

"Neither of you have said anything about this date you had. Which means one of a small handful of possible scenarios."

Scott shook his head, "I can't wait to hear this. Okay, go."

"One. It was terrible. You didn't get along, or worse, he stood you up. You two have already talked about it and agreed to never speak of it again."

"Plausible, all right, your other two options?"

"Two. The date was incredible. You laughed, you connected, but if that was entirely the case, you'd be with him now, and not sitting here with us, so something happened and you'll be seeing him later. If this is true, and we're not talking about it, then that means Scott is still jealous of you and doesn't want to hear about your love life."

"Interesting." I cocked an eyebrow at my roommate, who sneered at me. "Go on."

"Well, three is a real outlier. But the two of you have been super quiet all night long, which is kinda odd, so…you came home from your date. Scott was jealous. You two had a massive fight over it, but then realized how silly you were both being, made up…and—"

I stared at Scott wide-eyed.

"I knew it!" Amber pointed her finger toward me.

"Knew what?" Scott and I asked at the same time.

"You two still have a thing for each other. You fought and made up, like boners touching each other, sexual tension fixed and you both

80

glazed each other."

She wasn't entirely wrong, nor was she completely right. Scott and I hadn't fought, but damn did we ever have fun. My roommate hadn't lied. It had been a while for him. His load was so massive and thick it took me a full hour of combing my beard to get it all out. Thankfully a long hot shower and lots of soap rid me of any reminder of our afternoon fling.

On the flip side, poor Scott gagged hard enough to almost lose his lunch. I had been so caught up in the moment, with fistfuls of Scott's hair, I hadn't pulled back or warned him of my impending eruption. I actually had felt sorry for the guy. Scott just smiled and laughed after he had caught his breath and swallowed.

Despite the roomates and friends with benefits scenario, we still hadn't had a conversation about his dislike of Dominic. I wasn't going to be harsh, I just really needed to know why he had a hate on for the guy. Was he really still pining for me?

Scott broke the silence, "Okay, you're not wrong. But not right either."

"I told you, I'm psychic."

"Right. Okay. Here's the deal. Malik came home early. The date went well, but we were both horny, so we fixed it."

"Oh my god! Did you take pictures? Can I see?"

"No!" We both said, again at the same time.

"You guys are no fun."

"But you weren't right either."

"I totally was."

"Scott and I didn't fight, although, I am curious as to why you don't like the guy."

"Hey, I never said that." Scott retorted, then got up from the couch, went to the kitchen where we both heard the *pop, psss* of him opening another can of beer.

"But seriously, dude, you've made it pretty obvious you don't like him. That or Amber's right. You're jealous of me going out on a date."

"I am not jealous! Look, I'll admit, I'm not crazy about the guy. He gave me a really weird vibe at the bar the other night. I'm just looking out for you. You're my main guy, ya know? If there was something seriously wrong, I wouldn't have let you go on the date. I can't explain it. There's something just off about it all. That's all."

"Oh my god, you're so sweet." Amber said to Scott, then shifted her head to me, "Is he? Does he taste as sweet as I think he should?"

"Amber!"

"Look, I'm not getting any, from anyone. I need to live viacriously through you two."

"This conversation is over." Scott said with a middle finger in the air to emphasize his point, then returned to the couch, but sat next to me instead on the other side with our house guest. "Shove over, I'm sitting next to my bestie roommate."

Amber giggled, slid over and grabbed the remote. "Fine, but I'm your girl bestie, and for that, you have to watch Green Lantern with me."

"For the love of—" Scott was a superhero adicionado and that movie had not made the cut.

"Nope. Don't want to hear it. You won't spill the deets about your sexy-fun-times, I make you watch shit movies."

Scott elbowed me in the ribs. He was actually enjoying all of this.

After the movie, and a couple more drinks, we all headed off to bed.

As predicted, once Amber had staggered her way down the hall and passed out in Scott's room, he turned to me. "Can I sleep with you?"

I rolled my eyes, but nodded.

"Sweet." He leaned in and stole a kiss. He smelled and tasted like hops. Not a bad taste either.

I stood up, turned the TV off, and headed off to my bedroom, pulling off my shirt as I went. Scott was right behind.

Once we were naked, and in bed, Scott snuggled in tight to me and his readiness to revisit our afternoon tryst was all too apparent.

A small part of me wished that we were more compatible. Scott had always had my back, was a good guy, and well, damn. Under the covers, I wormed my hand in between our two bodies until I had a good grip on his shaft. Scott pulled away in order to grant me greater access, and with the addition room for movement, I stroked him.

"I love it when you do that."

"I know."

"Do it until I come?"

"As long as you return the favor. Just don't get it my beard this time."

"Promise."

"So, you really don't like Dominic?" I continued the back and forth motion. He was leaking and my fingers were getting slick. I was going to have to wash the sheets tomorrow.

Scott shuddered. "I can't believe you're talking about him while doing this to me." He chuckled.

"Are you jealous?" I stopped jerking him off and propped myself up on one elbow and looked him straight in the eye.

"No, I'm not."

"Good, 'cause that would be weird coming from the self-proclaimed poly guy."

"Okay, fair. Why'd you stop?" Scott reached down and found my rock hard dick, which wasn't nearly as big as his, but still ample enough for most, and reciprocated the motion. I closed my eyes giving in to the delightful feel of his caloused hands on such a tender part of my body. This time, I leaned in for a kiss.

I reached under the sheets for Scott, and picked up where I left off.

"Just be careful. Okay?" He asked of me and then tugged on my nuts, which I loved.

"Of course. If anything happens or starts to seem wrong, I'll immediately call it off and come home to you."

"Cool. You are my bestie bro. You know that, right? I'll always want you to be happier than me."

"Shut up." In the dim light of my bedroom, Scott wasn't going to see me blush, but the heat in my cheeks told me I was scarlet red. "Keep jerking. I could be close."

"Well in that case." Scott's eyes went wide as he disappeared under the sheets.

I gasped as Scott's wet mouth enveloped me.

PART 9

Dominic Ronove

Saturday, 4:40pm

Possessing a body isn't difficult. Most humans don't fight back, and frankly those that do aren't the ones you want to take up residence in. You end up expending more energy trying to win over the host than actually using it for your own purposes.

My current meat sack no longer fought. Hell, as I slipped back into it, which was like stepping into comfy house slippers, I would have sworn, on some level, it was happy to have me back. After all, there aren't a lot of corpses that get to stay topside for a few hundred years.

Regaining motor functions and senses indicated the slide back into my tall, muscular, and dark shell was successful. I heard the distinctive purr of my Benz which meant Rodolfo had once again found me.

"My god man, you have impecable timing." I grumbled out from behind clenched teeth. A welcoming body or not, sliding in and out of a skin shell takes a toll. I shook my head to get it right. "How do you manage to show up when I need you?"

"A talent?"

"Yes, well, whatever it is, I'm thankful for it. That house there." I pointed to the witches lair while trying to sit up. "The young female body in the kitchen. I need her alive, but however you need to do it, get her to the remote office, strung up, over a containment circle."

"Yes, boss."

Without any time to waste, I hoisted myself up, brushed off grass and dirt from my slacks, and followed behind Rodolfo's long-legged strides into the old victorian. Down the hall and into the kitchen we found Miles hunched over the young witch, salivating. Literally, strings of drool running out of his mouth.

"Hungry, or horny?" I was slightly disgusted.

"Can't decide."

"Either way, no, bad dog. Now, where's this gifted book? The one they used to summon me. The one you say has the lingering stench of another demon? I cannot leave that behind."

"Upstairs."

"Rodolfo, you can deal with this?"

"Yes, boss. What do you want me to do with the other one?"

"Ah, Mrs. Winterfield. Leave her. She'll set the stage nicely for when the siblings return." I turned to the hell hound, "Show me." I flicked my finger in front of me. A command of sorts that said to the mutt, "Lead the way".

The wiry blond lept up the stairs. I would have chalked that up to youthful exuberance, but I knew better. Miles was much older than I was. We climbed the stairwell, which was fairly steep, up not one but three flights until we reached what would have originally been the attic. A section of the house that would not have been used back in the day.

Sometime during the life of this home the room beneath the rafters had been re-engineered for habitation, complete with a drywalled ceiling and not the joists or exposed wiring and ducting I had expected. One would assume there had been insulation stuffed up there as well.

The room was a fair size, with only a small window on one side, but beneath the glass pane a padded window bench had been outfitted with several throw cushions and a nearby pie crust table allowed a guest to place a beverage or book on its scalloped surface. A cozy spot for a late afternoon, and a good read.

"Find it." I barked, Miles morphed into his hellhound form. The dog slinked around the room, its nose working over time.

It wasn't until I had my hand on the door jam when I noticed a prickling sensation. It wasn't pleasant. Like tiny needles digging into my flesh. Something was off about this room and it wasn't the fact that I had been born of shadows and the witches were light and sweetness. Obviously, intruding into a white witch's hen house would give me the heebie-geebies. No this was different. There was something else here.

Cerberus lifted his head, turned and sprinted across the room toward me, placed a palm on my chest and pushed me back through the doorway. He let out a single ruff as if to say, "No."

A simple and quiet bark was the last thing I heard before the room erupted in a blue-white light.

Holy light.

A kind of radiance bright enough to send creatures like me hurtling back to the depths of the pit. I threw myself to the side, away from the door, my back against the far wall, with my arm hoisted up and shielding my eyes from the explosion of purity.

But before I closed my eyes, Cerberus's head poked out from the doorway, his paws half morphed back into hands as he dug into the floorboards frantic to escape. His head lit up from the inside out as the blinding light permeated his skull. His muzzle twisted in pain as skin blistered, bubbled and melted away before me. Drips of flesh steamed and sizzled as they dropped onto the hardwood floor. With a throbbing pulse of bright white goodness, Cerberus flesh and bone was consumed until only the black amorphous energy that made up the souls of all demons fell to the floor. As the shining angel beams died, Cerberus disappeared.

"Well, shit. What the hell am I going to tell Malik about my damn dog." My head hung as I grit my teeth. "Fucking witches."

"Boss?" Rodolfo's voice came from several feet down the stairwell. It startled me, but Rodolfo couldn't see me, and I'd never let him see me unguarded.

"Yes?"

"We should go."

"Shit." I was shaking. That was two times in one weekend where I had come close to meeting my demise. No witch, demon, angel or any other monster had every achieved such a feat.

We were also leaving without the book. I still had no idea where it was in this room and currently entering the chamber was off limits, unless I wanted to join Cerberus.

I needed my greedy demon paws on that tome. There was no way I was leaving it intact and in the hands of white witches. Who knew what other bullshit they'd find in it and use against me. And without the book of spells I had no way to trace back who had given it to the little cunts. And now…now I needed to know which of my colleagues was attempting to do me in.

I had lost the creature that was going to be able to sniff out the traitor from within my own ranks. My head hurt trying to quickly devise a multifaceted plan that would net me this increasingly important magical spell book, eliminate the white witches for good, and determine who amongst my cohort was trying to do me in.

But I knew I couldn't do this without manipulating the two male siblings of the witch I now had captive.

"Did you leave a note?" I turned on the stairwell to face Rodolpho.

"On Mrs. Winterfield."

"Time and place?"

"Yes."

Damn Rodolfo was good. He had earned himself some additional compensation. Along with my scheming plans, I added an item to my mental to do list – Reward Rodolfo.

"Then let's go. I've had enough of this place."

"Did you stipulate the correct time?" I asked Rodolfo while sitting in the back seat of the Benz. He had already poured me a bourbon. A triple, on ice. It was going down far too easily.

"Your usual."

"Eleven eleven. It has a certain ring to it. A poetry of time, don't you think?"

"Yes, boss."

As much as I valued Rodolfo's service, and as good as he was, he didn't really carry our conversations very far. He was the dutiful "Yes" man. But I couldn't complain. He did his job well. In fact, more than well. He excelled.

"Drop me off at home, please. I'll shower, change clothes and meet you out there."

"Very well." Rodolfo swung the car around and changed directions. I heard the *thump* of the witch rolling in the trunk. That brought a smile to my face.

Rodolfo pulled up to my building, got out, walked around the car then opened the door for me. I left the interior of the car, and an empty tumblr. Buttoning my coat as I walked toward the building, our doorman met me outside the building and opened the door for me.

"Working on the weekend again Mr. Ronove?"

"I'm always working, Leslie."

"You need to take a break and have some fun. All work and no play. You know the expression?"

"I do." Play. Well, I had wanted to play with Malik. Perhaps after I had finished up with the nasty business of these witches I could focus a little time on Malik. I could play with him.

As I entered my apartment, Elisha sat at my desk. With pen in hand she was scribing out blank contracts. Boiler plate agreements that we could alter at a moment's notice. She lifted her head, placed the antique fountain pen on its holder, an outstretched human hand that had shriveled and dried over the years. The severed appendage almost looked like pure bone.

The pen had been a gift. It was carved from the femur of the Magnificent Suleiman, who once ruled the Ottoman Empire. He had sold his soul to me for the greatest of conquests, to rule the world.

He got his wish.

I got a pen, and a soul.

That pen had been used many times. Its tip had been dipped into the most dispicable pools of blood and signed some of the most devious souls to hell's domain.

"You look like you've had a very long day." Elisha quipped as she pulled back her long afro blown out hair. Her dark skin tone shone where the candellight's flickering flame illuminated the desk space.

"You're going to ruin your eyes if you try to work in this shitty light. We have electricity. You can use it." I flicked on a light, illuminating the master chef style kitchen that I never used. One of my massive gothic style desks sat in what would have been the dining room.

I don't eat. At least, not on a regular basis. And it's not required. Elisha and Rodolfo do, but they typically don't eat together, and the granite surface of the kitchen island sufficed for solitary meals.

"That's harsh," Elisha shielded her dark eyes from the glaring bulbs of the monstrous crystal chandelier that hung over the island. "I like candellight. It's romantic."

"Romantic? While scribing out the contracts I use to garner souls?"

"Yes."

"You are twisted."

"You're also avoiding my question. Why do you look like you've been dragged through a grave?"

"Witches."

"Again?"

"Yes."

"But they're dead now, right?"

"Not yet." I mumbled, clearly irritated as I walked over to the desk and stood behind Elisha. I peered over her shoulder to scrutinize her work. "Your penmanship gets better every year." I grabbed a corner of the parchment. It was very old. Made from the thinnest skins.

The swoops and curves of the contract's words swayed and danced across the scroll. Of course I would save special contracts such as these for much higher level agreements. A common soul would never warrant using such artwork as this.

"I think this is one of your best."

"Thank you, Mr. Ronove." Elisha let her head rest against my stomach as she leaned back. I cupped her chin and held her close. She would always be one of my favorites, and she was special. "The witches will be dealt with soon? You're not in any danger, though, right?"

"No, my dear. We will be fine. Rodolfo is at the remote office setting things up. I will meet him there later."

"Spirit hour?"

"Yes, quite. I do get the best results then." My staff knew me well. Eleven, eleven. Either in the morning or just before midnight was an auspicious time. Depending on which psychic, or witch, or preternatural being you asked, they'd give you different meanings. But the four ones when lined up to tell the time created two condiuts. Gates if you will. A way to commune with the dead. And after all, I dealt in death. I'd always had good luck with anything that had been done on 11:11.

"Take me?" Elisha snuggled up against my palm.

"No. It will be dangerous, and you know I cannot risk losing you."

"You never take me anywhere."

"I fear that is true. I should remedy that. But not tonight."

"Can I be of any other service for you?" I knew what Elisha was asking for, and she was always willing to give it, but a good dicking before such an important evening had proven to be a dangerous distraction for me. I might be a tad superstitious, but I wanted and needed all my energy for what would happen later. And besides, since meeting the handsome topaz-eyed, Malik, he was the only one I could picture sharing my bed.

I bent over and kissed Elisha on the forehead, "No darling. Not tonight. You are free to retire as you wish."

Elisha briefly looked disappointed, but then stood, turned and faced me, did a slight courtesy coupled with a nod of her head, then smirked and cocked an eyebrow as she turned and sauntered towards her bedroom.

I watched until she disappeared behind a closed door.

I wanted a very hot shower, a close shave on my neck and cheeks and a trim to my beard, a clean suit and a smart tie before I left to fix the mess the witches had left behind.

I still needed a game plan to get the book.

PART 10

Dominic Ronove
Saturday, 11:00pm

I like driving.

The sensation of moving at rapid speeds while calmly sitting behind a steering wheel is one small pleasure I too often let Rodolfo take on for me. Occasionally though, like tonight, a soothing ride to a victim's final destination is a perfect way to prep my mind for the work that lay before me.

I flexed my hand in front of the hangar doors, my remote office, and without actually touching the metal they peeled apart, screeching as unseen hands ripped them open. The shriek of the steel doors sent shivers down my spine.

The interior of the warehouse had been done up right.

I really needed to do something extra special for Rodolfo.

The interior of the warehouse had been lit by candels. Hundreds and hundreds of candels. This wasn't our normal fare, but for a witch who was going out, it was perfect. Hanging from the center joist of the hangar, by a long chain ending in a huge meat hook, dangled Riley. She squirmed once she saw me walking confidently toward her.

Rodolfo had stripped her so she wore nothing but her bra and panties. She was gagged, but her hair was still tied back in a pony tail, which was good, I wanted her to see everything.

"Riley, it's so very nice that you could come see us." See, I can have a sense of humour.

Riley mummbled something incomprehensible. I chuckled.

Reaching out I pulled down her gag. She snapped at me.

"Now, now. Biting me is not in your best interests. I assure you."

"You bastard. My brothers and I will send you back to where you belong, foul beast!" She spat at me, but missed.

"You're a fiesty little thing, aren't you?" I turned away from her and walked toward the outside wall where Rodolfo had set up my work table. It was one of those stainless carts on wheels. Something you'd have seen in a surgical suite. A black leather satchel lay on top of the gleaming surface. I pulled the table closer to where Riley hung.

Releasing the buckle on the satchel allowed me to flip it open, exposing a glorious set of instruments I had collected over the years. Various blades, needles, a very long pair of pointed pliers, a bone hammer, a couple of saws. All the things you'd need to make someone talk.

"Now, Riley, it has come to my attention that you were given a very special book. One that apparently you and your siblings took great interest in, studied up real good, and then tried to use the spells in it to send me packing.

"Just so you know, that won't be happening. I have a set amount of time I'm allowed to be here and," I glanced at my watch, "that time hasn't elapsed yet. In fact, I have several more centuries before I'm due back at the feet of my deviant Lord.

"So, futile as your attempt was, I also can't have such books loose on the world. I need to know who gave it to you."

"I'm not telling you shit."

"For a white witch you have a very nasty mouth. Let's see." I turned to my table and scouted the various implements available to me. "I do believe being obstinate and difficult should probably start with a loss of some minor body parts."

"What?"

I held up a rather horrid looking pair of tinsnips. They were old. I had procured them from the creator of the Choke Pear, a nasty device inserted into the mouth, or other orifices, then sprung open releasing sharp metal blades. Palioly had gifted me his sharpest snips in 1639 in exchange for some additional victims to perfect his toy and a couple bags of coin. With use over the years they had grown rusty, but had proven very useful. They were one of my favorites. I opened and closed them a few times, the blades making a sharp *snip snip*.

"Ah, there it is." I could smell her fear. Inhaling deeply, the cold sweat sheen on her body emerged almost instantly, her skin glowing from the moisture in the warm radiant candel light. "Now, let's try that again. I'll ask you a question, and you'll answer it. If I don't like the answer, you lose a finger or a toe up to a knuckle. We'll start with little pieces first. That's fair. Right?"

"Who gave you the book?"

"Fuck you."

"So mote it be. I believe those are the words your kind likes to use, yes?" I opened the tinsnips and made sure they made a nicely audible *snickt*. Then I evaluated my options. Her hands were tied and strung up over her head, making them out of reach of my snips. Her feet were bound together, and after hanging for as long as she had, I couldn't

96

imagine she had much energy left to kick. "I think a toe. But not the big toe. It is surprising how much people bleed when they lose it, and it's the balancing toe. Did you know that? If you lose your big toe your body has a hard time with balance and walking and stuff like that. You'd have to learn how to walk again. And that seems a bit extreme. Maybe the pinky toe? The little piggy that went wee wee wee. Yes, I like that idea."

I knelt down, pulled her feet across my knee, and jammed the open snips in between the toe.

"Last chance, Riley. What's it going to be?"

"I'm not telling you anything."

"Oh dear."

SNIP

Riley screamed.

I got up with the severed toe in hand, walked over and with a clean rag that was also in the satchel, wiped the blade off. I put the snips back on the work table.

"Now, that wasn't too bad, was it?"

Riley was still screaming.

I did tell you I hate loud noises, right?

"Riley, I'm not fond of screaming. I know that hurt, but if you don't stop screaming, I'll have to make you stop."

"You're an asshole. You fucking beast."

"Oh stop. Now you're just using flattery."

Riley glared at me with death in her eyes. My death. But she wasn't going to get that.

Here's an interesting piece of advice. Witches cannot do magic when under duress. As long as I kept the girl in pain, uncomfortable, tied up, and frantic, there was no way she was casting any spells on me.

"Let's try again." This time I walked over to my table and choose a delightfully sharp scalpel. "Riley, who gave you the book?"

"I will never tell you."

"Riley, do you know what happens when I cut into your skin and shape the incision into demon marks?"

Riley's eyes went wide.

"That's right. When you heal, if you get the chance to heal, the scars will be permanent marks on your skin. So, depending on what I carve into your hide, I could render you magicless, or perhaps vulnerable to posession. Really, there's no limit."

"Please, don't." Riley's eyes were wide in terror. Despite the pain, my latest tactic had captured her attention.

"Oh, see, there you go. There's the dint in the armour. Now, who was it."

Riley whimpered. I opened and closed the tin snips a few times.

"Mammon. It was Mammon. Oh god, please just let me go."

My eyebrows raised. Mammon was one of the four kings of Hell, bent on greed. Seems as if his wonton need to lay his paws on everything had once again expanded topside. Not like he hadn't been here before, but Lucifer kept him on a short leash. After all, once Mammon got his filthy fingers into a pie, it turned rotten. He had no class or couth. It was about hoarding and collecting. The one with everything wins.

I couldn't let that happen, now could I?

The amount of chaos I can create is far more delictable. Sadly, not all demons think alike.

"I see. And what is my frightening brother hell bent on this time?" I poked the edge of the blade up against Riley's ribcage. Thin skin there. I pushed the tin snips in, ensuring she'd feel the sharp bite of the pointed end.

She flinched away from the blade.

"He...he...please don't cut me."

"I make no promises." I pressed the blade into her skin just enough for it to start to cut.

Riley whimpered. "Tell me. What does my wayward and disallusioned brother want?"

"He wants you shackled at the feet of Lucifer where apparently you belong."

"I'm assuming those are his words." Regardless, they pissed me off. With a flick of my wrist, the blade cut deep into the thin skin.

Riley screamed again.

"Ah, ah, ah," I waved the bloody knife in front of her face, "Remember what I said? I don't like noise."

Her screaming subsided into a whine. Not much better, but certainly more tolerable. Blood leaked out from the cut, dripping down her side.

I went over and placed the snips on the table, after wiping it with the cloth.

I picked up a short, but very sharp drill bit. It took me a minute to get it fastened into my cordless drill, but the *whir* of the motor caught Riley's attention.

"Now that we know who gave you the book, I need to know where the book is, exactly. Absolute exact location in that fucking white light room of yours." I pulled the trigger on the drill. The auger bit spun and glinted in the candel light, complete with a grinding whine of the motor.

"You'll never get the book out of that room. Anything dark will erupt in flames. It's the way the house was built. My grandmother did it. I have no way of turning it off."

"Shame. Did you know that you can drill a hole in your lower arm and legs and cause incredible pain but not lasting injury or death?"

"Oh god, please..."

"God has nothing to do with it. Hasn't for years."

The metal doors of my remote office wrenched open with a horrid squeal as Rodolfo escorted Riley's two siblings in.

"Is it time already? I was just starting to have fun." I pulled the trigger on the drill again to empahsize the point. The brothers stopped in their tracks and then quickly scanned their hanging sister.

"Riley, are you okay?" The blond one said. Not the brightest.

"Does it look like she's okay? A crossroads demon has your sister dangling from a meathook. She's bleeding, and my bodyguard has escorted you both into my lair. Oh, and just so you know, this place is demon hexed out the ass to prevent you little weasels from casting any shitty spells." I put the drill down on the table, then flicked my arm up and over my head.

The interior of the hangar illuminated by the hundreds of glyphs, and wards, and script Rodolfo and I had spent weeks etching and painting into the metal clad structure after we had procurred the site.

The marks weren't anything they would have seen before. It might have been remotely similar to angel writing, but demon scratch is edgier, a little more rustic. I've been told it gives a certain chill to those who've never laid eyes on it.

The boys looked around awestruck, their mouths hung slack-jawed.

"So, now boys. Here's the deal. I want the book Mammon gave you." Rodolfo's eyes went wider than the boys' had been when I said *that* name. "And, one of you will be signing this." I snapped my fingers and one of Elisha's beautifully scripted parchment contracts appeared in my hand.

"Don't! Don't either of you dare." Riley screamed from her elevated position.

"Or," I turned, and with parchment still in hand, I grabbed my drill, pressed the button and delighted in the looks of horror on the siblings faces.

"Let her down." Noah said.

"Book first."

"That's going to take me at least an hour to get!"

"Well then, best you'd hurry. I understand being hung from your hands like that can do some terrible damage to your rotator cuff." I shooed the boy away. "Now, Grayson, what will you and I discuss while your brother is otherwise occupied?"

Noah let out a short primal scream, scowled at me and Rodolfo, then turned and jogged out of the hangar. As soon as he was out of sight, I replaced the gag on Riley, and turned to Grayson, "So, here's the deal. Book, signed contact, and I let you sister go free. Yes? Noah's going to get the book, all you have to do is sign this. I'll leave it right here for you, with a lovely pen. All you have to do is jab yourself with the nib. It'll take your blood as ink, and then you sign. Easy. Right? I'm going to leave Rodolfo here to watch over you and your sibling. I have a quick little errand I need to do."

Rodolfo had been standing a few feet away, playing the role of not only chauffer, but also kidnapper and bodyguard. He was such a loyal employee. I leaned into his ear as I got near to him, "The symbol I taught you? Remember?"

Rodolfo nodded once.

"Good man. For every minute that ticks by, you carve a line into the flesh of that witch. Understood?"

Another nod.

"Perfect. I'll be back, as soon as the hex mark is finished."

I strode out to the exit, casting a side-eye at Grayson who watched me leave with the attention of a mouse watching a hunting cat leave the vacinity. As soon as I passed through the metal doors the night air washed over me. Its clean briskness rushed across my face, clearing my head and erasing the stress of the last hour.

I closed my eyes and inhaled, enjoying the momentary serenity.

"Now, where do we suppose Noah is?" I squinted, glanced around until I honed in on his presence and willed myself to be there.

A blink of an eye, and I was sitting in the car with Noah.

"Is this as fast as you can go?"

Noah jumped, hard and fast, inadvertantly placing his hand on the car's horn. The blasting sound made me grimace.

"Jesus, shit!" Noah yelled.

"Now now, boy. There's no need to be using such language. Here's the thing. I don't have time to wait for an hour while you dilly dally attempting to retrieve this book of yours, and frankly, I don't trust you to not come back with some idiotic plan to try and exorcise me out of the topside. Not that you can do that, but damned if you won't try. Your kind always tries. So this is what I'm going to do for you.

"The method I used to get here in this car, I can take a passenger. It will speed things up. And just think, maybe your sister won't bleed to death or lose the use of her arms because she's been in that god-awful position now for at least a couple of hours.

"All you need to do is sign this." I snapped my fingers and another sheet of Elisha's lovely scroll work appeared.

"What is that."

"Really? You're not that dumb, are you?"

"What is it?" The car swerved violently to one side as Noah glared at me, then glanced down at the parchment skin.

"For hell's sake, pull over before you crash and kill yourself. You won't be good to anyone then."

Noah did as instructed. Perhaps he wasn't as stupid as I thought.

"It's a contract, my dear boy. You get six years. Six peaceful, restful years free from demonic activity and any other type of hellish invasions, in exchange for the book and your sister. You don't sign the contract, and the big oaf that was with me tonight get's to have your sister. And he doesn't like them when they're alive and kicking. Prefers things a little on the colder side – if you get my drift."

"You wouldn't."

I simply stared at him. What a stupid statement. I took back my earlier assumption on his intelligence quotient.

"I would."

"Damnit." Noah punched the steering wheel, then hung his head. I took that as my indication I had won.

"Here's a pen."

It's odd how fast siblings will sign their lives away for one of their own. Now granted, not every sibling, just the close ones, and these three were thick as thieves and I had guessed correctly. The first sibling to rush out and grab the book would be the one who would give in first and the easiest.

If I had played my cards right, Rodolfo was carving a demon hex mark into the flesh of the witch, as Grayson remained defiant. But every minute he stayed stoic, his stubbornness rendered the most powerful witch in their family magically impotent. I was currently witnessing sibling number one sign his soul over to me in exchange for his sister, and the book of evil deeds, while Rodolfo would be forcing sibling number three into signing a second contract, but waiting until it was too late to save his sister's abilities.

Problem solved.

Two souls signed in one night and the most powerful witch of the three of them left scarred and powerless.

Once I had my signed contract, I zapped Noah and myself over to the house, waited for him to retrieve the book, then took us both back to the warehouse.

Upon entering the hangar, Rodolfo handed me the second contract, and displayed his rather deeply carved sigil on the back of the girl's knee.

"That's an interesting spot." I scrunched up my eyebrows.

"Pain point." Rodolfo replied while cleaning the blade, which was curved on the end, meant for scooping out flesh. The sigil was deep. If the girl tried to remove the mark it would be extremely painful and most likely cause muscle damage.

"Nicely done." I nodded once and patted Rodolfo on the shoulder. He seemed quite pleased. He then went over to the winch on the wall and cranked it until Riley was considerably less high than she currently was, and allowed me access to her binds.

"Now boys," I grabbed a long serrated blade from my leather satchel which made both change their stances into a guarded position, as I swiped just above their sister's hand. "Collect your things and go. And do *not* attempt to thwart me ever again, or I will call in those contracts so fast your soul will spin."

Riley fell from the meat hook and crumpled onto the concrete floor. The puddle of blood that had collected at her feet meant she slipped as her feet came into contact with the slippery goo that had already started to congeal. The resounding smack as her head hit the floor made even me bite my bottom lip.

"Oops." I said.

The boys rushed over to assist their sister.

My work was done. With a wave of my hand, the three white witches were sent away. Where they ended up, I couldn't say, nor did I care at the moment. They were out of my hangar.

"Clean up?" Rodolfo asked.

"Yes, please." I grinned.

The rest of my night consisted of a drive home. But all the while I drove, being rather happy with myself that I had resolved this ugly situation, I spied the nasty book that sat in the passenger seat, I couldn't get the thought of Malik out of my head.

I glanced at the clock. It was late. Close to one in the morning. But is was a Saturday night, and Malik was a young and handsome creature.

"Oh why not." I pressed the audio command button on my steering wheel. "Call Malik."

The computer system worked it's hoodoo magic, and dialed the number.

I listened intently while the phone rang, and rang, and rang.

Ah well, I guess not everything was going to go my way.

I had almost hit the red 'hang up' button when a racous burst of laughter could be heard over the speaker, followed by a, "Hello?"

"Malik?" I said.

"Dominic, is that you?"

"It is. My apologies for calling so late, but I just wrapped up my business for the night. I left you so rudely this afternoon. I was hoping maybe you'd still be up for a nightcap? I know it's late. If it's not a good time, we can do it another time."

"No, I—" There was more laughter coming in from where ever he was. "I'm sorry about that." I could hear a door shut. "I'm over at a friend's place. They're having a party, and after you said you were busy tonight, I just figured —"

"No, no, of course. That's fine. A young handsome guy like you needs to be out enjoying himself."

"Um, why don't you come here?"

"To a party at your friend's place?"

"Sure. Why not?"

"Well, I might be overdressed." I glanced down at my suit, trying to tell if there was any blood splatter on it.

"No one will care. Especially if you're coming straight from work."

"Well, I suppose. Sure, why not. It'll give me a chance to have that drink with you."

"Awesome. I'll text you the address."

Guess I was going to a party packed with inebriated young humans. I hadn't been to such feast in years.

My mind wandered through fond times in ancient Rome, and then conjured up an image of Malik in a toga.

My meat suit seemed happy and pleased with this turn of events.

PART 11

Malik Parsa

Sunday, 1:00am

"Who was that?" Scott popped up in front of me after I left the privacy of the bathroom where I'd just finished talking to Dominic.

"Oh, well if I tell you, it'll spoil your mood." I raised an eyebrow and gave my roommate a mischevious grin.

Scott rolled his eyes, "Oh, *him*. Seriously dude, I really don't care."

"That's one hundred and ten percent a lie. I've known you forever. The one thing you can't do is lie."

"Okay, sure. You're wrong though. I can lie, and I do care. All I'm saying is be careful. I just get a funny vibe from him. I don't want to see my best buddy get hurt. Besides, if you went suddenly missing, I'd never get any good head." Scott elbowed me in the ribs.

I laughed. We had had a good time recently. Nothing we hadn't done before, or that was out of the ordinary for us. In fact, in some ways our tryst had been overdue. Our extra level of friendship bonded us. I honestly believed Scott and I were as close as two human beings could get.

I trusted him implicity, and had done so for so many years I knew he'd never do anything to hurt me.

"Where's Amber?" I asked, having not seen her for at least an hour. Now that was weird. Since we had become friends Amber had been with us almost constantly.

Scott shrugged. We both decided we would split up and look around and find her.

We'd been invited to the party by Sung, the bartender and one of the coolest guys from *The Common*. The house address he gave us was in Old Glenora, not far from where Dominic and I had lunch the day before. Normally I wouldn't have spent any time in this neighborhood. I didn't belong. I came from the wrong side of the tracks for the people in this tax bracket. Sung was still working the bar, but said he'd see us as soon as he locked the doors.

I glanced at my watch.

It wasn't even two in the morning yet, so Sung wouldn't be here for a couple more hours.

The house was sprawling, old, and every corner you turned led to a new historical discovery. Lights that had been turned on were dim, casting a yellow pallor over the wallpapered walls.

On my search for Amber I had ambled down a particularly long and gloomy hallway, pictures of Edmonton's beginnings dotted the walls. Blue collar men, dusty and dirty, hard worked, and underpaid were framed in various poses outside the entrances to mines.

Old pick axes and helmets adorned the wall alongside the pictures. I had forgotten that Edmonton's river valley had many abandoned mines.

The house dripped in nostaligia.

The air seemed heavy in here, like the weight of all the hundred and twenty years since the picture had been taken permeated every atom surrounding me. I leaned in closer to examine one image. The guy was unbelievably good looking, despite the quality of the photo, which wasn't the greatest. But this guy was dressed more like a businessman. Miners stood all around him.

Maybe the founder?

"Hey, I found her." Scott appeared at the end of the hallway and beckoned to me. I followed until we stood in the kitchen. Amber was laughing hysterically while sitting at the kitchen table with another girl.

She was thin. Almost too thin. She had a black lace shawl draped over her shoulders and a floppy garden hat obscured most of her face. Her arms were covered in various tattoos, mostly black ink with swirls and spirals forming skulls and roses. Large bangles dangled from her wrist, along with leather ties and the typical friendship bracelets. Her long flowing tie-died skirt done up in dark brown and oranges lay wrapped around her legs, its edge trimmed out in a similar lace akin to the spider's web-like cover she pulled closer around her.

Amber's gaze caught us staring at her from the kitchen's opening into the hallway.

"Oh my god, you have to meet these guys. They are the coolest! My besties." Amber slapped her hand down on the table. She was lit. Pickled. Soaked in booze. Tomorrow would be a tough haul for her. "Guys, c'mere!" She waved us over.

Scott and I looked at each other, then approached cautiously.

"Regina, this is Scott – the hairy, sexy, woodsman, and this hottie beast is Malik. It's okay, they're totally gay. But they're not a couple!

Just besties," then Amber leaned in closer to Regina, and although she meant to be quiet as she put her hand up to her cheek to shade her mouth from anyone's view, said rather loudly, "but they had sex with each other today."

Amber broke out into a side-splitting laugh, complete with tears streaming down her face. Apparently, she was the only one who found the whole thing funny. Regina hadn't laughed, and I could feel the heat rippling off of Scott's body he was so embarrassed.

I chose to ignore everything and extended my hand forward, "Hi Regina, I'm Malik. It's nice to meet you."

She tilted her head at me and squinted, then carefully, if not gingerly, took my offered hand and gave it a curt shake.

She was deathly cold. Her lace wrap wasn't going to keep her nearly warm enough.

"It is interesting to meet your acquaintance." Regina replied, which made me pull back slightly.

What an odd thing to say.

Regina stood up and nodded at me once, glared at Scott, then disappeared down the hall we had entered into the kitchen.

"Okay, she's a freaky bitch." Scott chimed in while putting his hands on Amber's shoulders. He leaned over, "You, my dear, are wasted."

"Hell's yes!" From somewhere near her, Amber had grabbed a shot-glass that was full of something and in one jerky, alcohol laden motion, swigged it back.

"Okay, well, I don't think you need any more of that, or tomorrow you're gonna wish you were dead."

"Ptthhbbt." Amber stuck her tongue out at both of us. Then she giggled incessantly.

"Oh boy. She's gonna be a handful." I was just about to suggest we call her a cab when a warm hand gripped my shoulder. I looked up at Scott who eyed the person behind me with an unfriendly face. Without even turning around, I knew exactly who it was. "Dominic, you came."

An aroma of musk, cedarwood, and leather enveloped me – clearly from Dominic's cologne. I could feel him lean in close as his whiskers tickled the back of my neck.

"Come with me?" He asked, politely.

"Sure." I got up. He took me by the hand and led me down a hallway I wasn't sure I had been down yet, and pulled me into the closest room, abandoning Scott with Amber. Dominic closed the door, then pushed me up against the wall.

We were in a bedroom, and its décor was in line with the rest of the state of the house. Antique, ancient, and awkwardly like Grandma's house. Dominic leaned in close and kissed me. His mouth was warm, almost hot, and he tasted sweet like fresh water.

"Hi to you too." I had to pull away to catch my breath. I had been hoping for this kind of private time with him.

"So, who invited you to the party?" Dominic asked then licked my neck.

"Sung, from the bar." I shuddered in delight.

"Mmm." He replied. "So, as much fun as this is, I'd very much like to take you away from here and have some alone time with just you. What do you think? Would that be a welcome invitation? I am happy to drive your friends to wherever they need to be."

The erection in my pants throbbed hard.

What is it about this guy?

"I am absolutely open to that invitation. How about I go back and find them and let them know we're gonna take off?"

"Make sure you also extend my offer to drive them home?"

"Of course!" I peered at Dominic from half-lidded eyes. "Why are you so damn perfect?"

"I'm not so sure I would grant myself such adjectives, but I'm flattered you think that way. I'll meet you by the front door."

I didn't really want to break away from him. His body was amazingly warm, even through his clothes. Perhaps it was the few drinks I had consumed that lowered my normal amount of composure, but Dominic and I had never been quite this close, and clearly my hormones agreed with his stunningly dark masculinity.

I grabbed each side of Dominic's head and pulled him toward me, kissing him enthusiastically, while allowing my hands to run over his cheeks, feeling the coarseness of his beard, then down his neck, across his massive shoulders and then over his very muscular back.

I was going to have a very good night.

Dominic Ronove
Sunday, 1:36am

The second I walked into the house I could smell death.

And then I spied Sahir, sitting in the corner of the living room in a char that could have been described more accurately as a throne, sipping a glass of what could only be blood. Sahir, the *basrahip* of the coven that owned and controlled *The Common*.

Sahir spied me from his perch, raised an eyebrow and nodded in my direction.

"*Welcome to my party, Ronove.*" The greeting echoed through my head. Vampires and telepathy. I had unknowingly stumbled into Sahir's nest.

Dammit.

I returned the nodding gesture.

At that moment I knew what this party was all about.

Food.

I had heard Sahir hosted these soirees every now and then. It was an easy way to find prey for the entire flock of his undead minions. Most of the humans who had stumbled into an unfortunate invite and were here past a certain hour would most likely meet their ends tonight. And knowing Malik and his friends were here meant I had to get them out. Now.

As I stood at the front door, waiting for Malik to collect his companions, Sahir approached.

"Dominic Ronove. It's been a spell." The man was stunning. Most vampires were, or minimally exuded a charm that was unrelenting. It was part of their own brand of magic. It assisted in the hunt for sustenance and guaranteed survival. Humans had no resistance to their charms and wiles. Sahir was old enough, and powerful enough that even I could feel his allure.

He wasn't large by stature, average you might say. But his sweeping thick locks of raven hair, expertly styled and cut, with the deepest brown eyes, pale skin and just the right length of stubble framed an undeniably striking face. Any human would have had a hard time saying no to the undead blood feeder. Gay, straight, somewhere in between – it wouldn't matter – he was *that* good looking. His outfit well represented the creatures of the night. Donned in all black, his vest was tight, accentuating his toned body. The vest, tailored of black velvet, with raised black paisley swirls, created a haunting look that was as daunting as it was beautiful.

As he spoke, his slightly elongated canines flashed white. His lips though, that was the tell. They were pale, almost ashen. That meant he hadn't been fed in a long time. A simple glass of bottled blood, charmed and stored so that it didn't coagulate would keep him alive, but it wouldn't satisfy him, or keep him virulent and robust.

"You just got here. Leaving so soon?"

"I'm afraid so. Just came to collect my…" What exactly was Malik? Certainly not a boyfriend, at least, not yet. A date? Perhaps. "My date."

"Malik. Yes, I've been told. How is it that a demon that scrambles for wayward humans, foraging for his master's food, is able to snag a delicious morsel the likes of which I haven't set eyes on in a millenia? How is that, Dominic?"

"Ah, well, if you must know, we met at your bar."

"Again, I heard. I have little sets of eyes everywhere. You forget that. What if I were to tell you that I would prefer if Malik stayed?"

I could see Malik and his two friends walking up behind Sahir. There would be no hiding anything from the monster. He was old enough to be able to track everything that went on within his domain.

"Well, the last thing I would ever want is to remove someone against their will. Let's ask, shall we?"

Malik's friend was holding up the girl who had accosted me at the bar the night I had met Malik…what was her name? Ember? Jade? No…Amber – that was it. And Amber appeared to be less than coherent.

"Malik, have you been introduced to your host this evening?"

Malik studied me carefully, then glanced over at Sahir, "No, I don't believe I have."

"Sahir Hamdi." The vampire smiled, extending a hand. See, we all follow human traditions for the sake of fitting in.

Malik reached for the hand, grasped it, and shook. But the minute his human skin touched vampire, that flash of recognition happened in his eyes. The same look he'd given me the night we made eye contact at *The Common*. Just a flash. If you weren't careful, you'd miss it.

Malik shifted. He seemed uncomfortable.

I pressed the matter. There are rules a vampire connot control and must adhere to. One, they can't enter a private domain without being invited. That much is true. But the same can be said about retaining guests. If the human hasn't been subdued and charmed by the creature first, and they no longer wish to reside within the undead's company, a simple request to leave, and the vampire must comply.

That was a little-known fact.

"Malik, I know I said I'd drive you and your friends home. Looks like Amber has reached her fun limit. But Sahir would prefer if we stayed. What would you like to do?"

I gave Malik a wink. Hopefully it was enough to convey to him how I wanted our evening to proceed. But ultimately the decision was his.

Sahir was seething. He knew exactly what I was doing.

"Oh!" Malik glanced between me and Sahir. I could tell he was doing mental leaps trying to find the right words to not insult his host. "Thank you, Sahir. You have a beautiful and most interesting home. I was enjoying the historical photos in the hall. But as you can see, I think my friend is about to pass out, and I would hate for her to ruin your rugs should she..." Malik made a grimace. "But perhaps another time! And besides, Dominic has offered us rides home, and that is an offer we can't turn down. Cabs are so expensive these days."

Malik gave Sahir a weak smile.

"Well, then I guess that settles it." I said with a smug sneer while staring at Sahir. I needed to assert a little dominance. After all, I might not be a reigning Prince of Hell, and I might ultimately work for them, but who knows. I might be there one day. And if I showed any weakness right now Sahir would have my flesh suit torn into ribbons before I could argue.

My open invitation to *The Common* might be in jeopardy though.

Nope. Best to wrap this up and get Malik and crew out of harm's way.

I nodded once to our host, opened the door, and pulled Malik out.

Getting Amber into my car was a chore. Thankfully she did nothing to ruin my upholstery.

After a very quiet fifteen-minute ride to Malik and Scott's apartment, it grew awkward when I didn't go in, and instead, Malik left with me.

"Your roommate looks like he was upset you are coming with me."

"Scott's being weird. Ignore him. He's fine. Besides, he'll be busy dealing with Amber."

"True." I wrapped an arm around Malik as he slid into the crook of my arm, next to me in my car. "My place, then?"

Malik raised his eyebrows and smiled. "That sounds like fun."

"I'm glad you think so."

PART 12

I had to stifle a grin as I escorted Malik into my apartment. From the nervous energy that rumbled off of him, and the distinct odor of excitement, Malik failed attempting to hide his enthusiasm. Admittedly, a growing intoxication – and not from anything I had imbibed – stirred within me. Getting to explore and hopefully taste every inch of this delicious creature would be the highlight of what had been a rather trying week.

I had placed a quick text on the elevator to make sure Rodolfo and Elisha were well out of sight. Having live-in staff could sometimes be… well, difficult.

"Holy, shit! Dominic, transaction business must be really fucking good. This is your place?" Malik took a few hesitant steps in through my front door. A faint whistle blew through his rounded lips. "Damn."

"Okay, well don't make a big deal of it. That just makes everything awkward." I winked at him. "I have been successful. I'm also rather pleased you like it. Some would say my taste in décor is rather—"

"Spooky, but cool as hell."

"Sure. I'll take that."

A grand tour of my dwelling was out of the question, but I pointed out the obvious destinations. "Kitchen is over there and you may help yourself to anything in the fridge. The central bathroom is right down that hall should you require it, however, my bedroom is over here." I pointed in the direction of my lair.

"That's the only room I want to see." Malik turned and nuzzled up to me getting as close as possible. I'd have rather been heading toward our intended destination. Instead, he wrapped his arms around my waist and burried his nose into my beard. "You smell so good."

"You are a very misbehaved creature. One I think I'm going to like getting to know." I let him cuddle in close.

Malik's body scent overwhelmed me with its headiness. His muscles were firm, his skin humanly warm, and even though he appreciated the way I smelled, the reverse was equally as true. Malik's closeness was a balm to my demonic nature. The air between us filled with our mingled bouquet, deep and rich in masculinity. Malik exuded hints of hot metal, engine oil, and summer night breezes, and when twisted with my own scents of worn leather, coal, and nightmare fear, a deadly concoction brewed. An alchemic potion of heady masculinity. They were equally odd aromas. Malik's though quickly became imprinted on me. It's uniquness a pleasure. I'm certain to some, the combination would have surely been offputting, but not for me. It was excitement and speed all wrapped up in a tasty, topaz-gold eyed youth.

I took his hand. "Come."

As I reached my bedroom, I had to drop Malik's hand in order to swing open the double doors to my chamber. The first section contained my private office, where my gothic deep-chestnut desk sat, surrounded with bookshelves filled with ancient tomes, scrolls, my day-to-day ledgers, and a fireplace – which again, Rodolfo had anticapted my needs and lit. On the otherside of that hellfire lay my bedroom. The grimoire recently acquired from the trio of witch siblings sat on top of my desk, waiting to be studied.

But the focus for the rest of the evening would be on Malik. I looked forward to getting him naked and exploring his humanity while the fireplaced burned with the blue-tipped flames from my birthplace.

Granted I couldn't let Malik wander aimlessly through my office, so I made light of it, but would have to ensure he didn't wander off or allow his eyes to get too close to any of the books in this room. "All my customers contracts. Paperwork for days. Boring as hell." I gave Malik a wink as he refocused in on the sound of my voice. His eyes were saucers as he took in what I'm sure he considered to be financial freedom. He wasn't wrong. But he also had no idea how it had been achieved.

"I need to rethink my career."

"Ah, well, don't be to rash about that. Remember I have to work almost twenty-four, seven. I wouldn't wish my job on anyone."

"But clearly it pays."

"It does, but fortune isn't everything, Malik. You have no idea how privileged I feel that I happened to be in the right spot, and the right time in order to meet you." As I guided him towards the other side of my room, I twirled him around so I could inspect every angle, enjoying every inch of him. When he came full circle, I stopped him, then tugged up on his T-shirt. His hands lifted into the air, granting me permission to remove the garment. Without diverting my gaze from his unearthly coloured eyes, I lay his top on the corner of my bed. Reaching out, and letting my fingers caress his chest. My tongue involuntarily licked my lips. His torso was taught and lean, covered with delightfully trimmed chest hair. "How fortuitous I am, indeed." I let my finger tip circle his nipple, then bent down to kiss it, lick it, and gently bite it.

Malik's hands grasped the back of my head, pushing my head into his body. I took that as a request to continue, so while torturing his now hard nub, and personally enjoying the scratch of his body hair against my lips and the feel of his hardened flesh between my teeth, I allowed my fingers to roam where they wanted.

His belt buckle was an unpleasant barrier. I fiddled with it, struggling to get the beastly thing to release. I had a deep need to grasp Malik's meat and weigh the heft of his balls.

Malik moaned as he ran his fingers through my beard. The boy was already thrusting, pushing his erection into my chest.

Youth and exuberance.

To my surprise, Malik pulled my head away, and then lifted me up. "You have far too many clothes still on you."

"Fair enough. Shall I, or would you like to do the honors?" I tilted my head, while I gazed into Malik's topaz and gold eyes, the dark outline of kohl around the iris made the contrast of colours quite stark, especially in the fire light of the room.

"You'll let me?"

"Of course." I stood still, stretching my arms out to my side, palms facing him. It was a gesture that implied access, allowing Malik free reign. He shuddered in anticipation but took the time to explore, deliberately extending the foreplay and the titilation we were both experiencing. As he ran his hot palm over my shirt covered chest, my stomach muscles twitched with delight. He smirked as he felt the jump of muscle, then slid his hand over my groin. He stopped when he felt the hardness and squeezed.

"I like."

"I'm glad."

Malik wasted no time in removing my shirt, which he paid much respect to by also laying it gently on the corner of the bed, alongside his own. He then unclasped my belt, with no problems I might add, undid the top button of my slacks, and slowly, almost tortuously unzipped me. With my pants released, he let them fall to the floor.

I rarely wear undergarments, and so I stood I front of him, naked, aroused, and ready to devour him. He cupped my sac in one hand, stroked me with the other, and leaned in to kiss me.

I trembled. It's not often a human makes a demon shiver with delight. He was firm with his grip, yet gentle in his actions. Fiend or not, the simple carress of Malik's touch, skin to skin would make almost any creature puddle with pleasure.

"Your arm is wrapped. Do you have a injury I need to be careful of?"

I had forgotten. The amount of craziness over the last couple of days had completely banished the need to heal my punctured arm.

"Hmph. You allowed me to completely ignore the pain. I wouldn't worry too much, but to be safe, maybe don't grab that arm?"

Malik chuckled, "I make no promises. I may lose control, but I'll try." He was still stroking me.

Interesting fact; even though the body I inhabited had been dead for well over a century, it still reacted as if it was alive. I burned hotter than normal – but that was the demon energy in me. I didn't bleed, as no blood needed to flow. I breathed, but only for appearances. However, most other bodily functions still occurred.

Including arousal, of which Malik continued to explore. Without missing a stroke, he leaned forward, running his free hand up my torso and letting his fingers drag through the untrimmed matt of hair covering me.

We kissed, his tongue flickering and dancing across my own. Gentle nibbles of my lower lip tempted me into returning more aggressive bites. I wanted to leave passion imprints on him with pointed fangs, and clawed nails to mark his flesh as mine, but resisted. Perhaps another time. This episode and its swells of highs beared repeating.

His breath was sweet, and tasted of innocence. Mine was assuredly anything but that, yet his embrace suggested he found me as irresistable.

Malik's roving hands left nothing undiscovered. I throbbed, with excitement and an enthusiasm I hadn't had in years, if ever.

I leaned into him, getting close to his ear, "You have far too many clothes still on." I turned his own phrase back on him. "May I?"

"Good god, yes please."

"There are no good gods in this place, I promise."

I could tell he didn't want to let go of me, but there'd be more time for touching as soon as his skin lay exposed. I needed him uncovered, visible, and vulnerable. I wanted to eat him alive and savor every morsel.

With a little assistance from Malik, I finally released his belt buckle, pulled down his jeans, and discovered he was wearing a black jockstrap that matched his black jeans. I pulled him forward. He melted in my arms, pressed up against my body.

"I want you." I said, slowly teasing the thin layer of remaining fabric off his body with my fingertips.

He stepped out of the underwear as they fell to his ankles.

"No need to ask. You may do whatever you'd like." Malik wriggled his hands down to my throbbing manhood which was nestled inbetween our bodies. Malik's shaft was rubbing against mine, as he grasped both of them in one fist.

I pulled back slightly, allowing him to stroke us both at the same time.

Standing upright was becoming problematic. My legs wobbled from the sheer ecstacy of our bodies pressed together, and Malik's unrelenting stroking. I wasn't pleased with my human shell for giving in so eagerly to these sensations.

But then, they were pleasures of the flesh.

Others have been damned for much less.

"Let's get on the bed."

Malik complied.

We were in the deepest part of night, a time where most souls are at rest, and those of us who belong to the darkness are often at our peak of consciousness, stirring the waters of nightmares and troubles, causing mayhem, perhaps creating a little destruction – but nothing from his world or mine would have distracted us.

We got lost in the sensation of each other. Tongues tasting whatever the other offered, hands grasping flesh, bodies rubbing, tussling, wrestling.

There were tickles, and slaps, carreses and bites.

A tug of war between intoxicating seduction and rapture coupled with the borderline tease of pain. We continued, until I could stand no more.

Flipping Malik over so that he was on his knees, I spread his legs out. Lubed and already relaxed and ready, I pushed into him.

We simultaneously groaned as I slipped into Malik's warmth. A slow steady push first until I was deep within him, a moments rest until I felt him relax and give in to me. I pulled back, then moved forward. Slow deep strokes, until a rhythm began. We moved in time with each other.

It didn't take too long though before my pace quickened and my grip on his hips tightened.

And then it happened.

I lost control – something I haven't done in many years. My sight expanded so that I was seeing into Malik's soul, reliving his history, and sensing him with my demonic touch. I knew my eyes would appear as solid black orbs. If he turned around, my nature would be lain bare.

Thank all the levels of hell he was facing away from me.

But the air became thick around us. Light crept out of the room escaping from my true form, deepening the gloom until the corners were lost in shadow. The very core of my being took over my human form, reshaping it so that my face distorted, horns grew, black veined-packed wings erupted from my back filling the room. They flapped and sputtered as my hips continued their rythmic motion.

The tips of my nails grew thick and sharp, digging into Malik's tender flesh.

And from deep within me, the yearning to be inside of Malik, to be so close to his very essence I would need to crawl into his skin, took over.

Reaching forward, my arm wrapped around Malik's chest, I pulled him up close to me. His breathing was laboured and heavy. But his moans and grunts of pleasure gave away his desire.

Malik's arms grabbed my thighs as he kept time with my movement. Flesh against flesh, hands grasped tightening muscles in anticipation of an inevitable end. He straightened, and stiffened, pushing himself onto me so that I could thrust no deeper inside him.

And then he came.

White light beamed out from his body, scorching hot. His form radiated light, spewing forth as energy throbbed and pulsated, illuminating from deep within his torso our coupled form threw shadows against the wall. His angelic body nestled deep within my winged beastial frame.

Once Malik's peak had been topped, he slumped forward onto his hands and knees. His breath labored. The light he emanated slowly subsided, pulsing dimmer with each heartbeat. I could see his ribcage and spine. I saw his heart beating far too fast.

And then I saw the brand in the center of his back. A symbol I'd seen before.

Archaic and ancient, but its meaning escaped me while in the thoes of passion.

It was a sigil few humans would have ever seen.

But I was too far gone. I couldn't stop. I couldn't pull out, I needed to finish.

I had to be inside him.

Light blinded me as it scorched through the crack between my blackout blinds, making me squint rousing my body.

As I attempted to prop myself up I was weighed down.

Malik was draped overtop of me.

As I stirred, his eyelids fluttered, then peeled apart.

He peeked at me through sleep filled eyes.

"Good morning."

I glanced over at my alarm clock.

"It's well past noon." Despite some foggy memories of the end of our coupling, I smiled at him, wrapped both arms around his waist and leaned in to kiss his forehead. "Would you like breakfast?"

"Are we having monster meat?" He shimmied a hand between my legs and grabbed my rock hard cock. Malik had a rather beastly affect on me.

I pulled the sheet back to expose us, suddenly feeling a bit too hot, then flipped Malik over so I was on top. His own erection grinding into my stomach.

"I don't know if I could ever say no to you. And that is very dangerous." I kissed him. But I meant it.

I wasn't sure what had happened last night, but one memory stood out. The brand I saw on his back.

I coerced Malik to flip over for me, allowing me to penetrate him again. But this was only to tease him. He was still wet from our actions hours earlier. It didn't take much to slide in.

Malik groaned, "Oh god, yes..."

Running my finger over the skin on his back, I traced out the brand that had been displayed last night. It was no longer there. Had I seen things? No, I was quite certain the welted flesh mark had been real.

I thrust a few times, gently, teasing him, but then pulled out, rolled him over, straddled him, and took us both into my hand.

"I think I'd like to watch you cum this time."

And that's how we spent the remainder of our afternoon. Wrapped up in each other, pleasuring one another, but I never let it get out of control.

I could never let myself lose control with him ever again. And thankfully, Malik seemed none the wiser for what had occurred.

I needed more time. Time with him, and time to research the brand that had mysteriously appeared on his back.

A niggle in my brain told me I already knew what the sigil meant.

After Malik left my company, sometime close to the dinner hour, I walked into my bathroom needing to clean myself up. As I stood naked in front of the mirror, the wrap around my punctured arm had come loose.

As I unwound the bandage, I was shocked to discover my wound no longer existed. The hole had completely disappeared, and the black ooze that typically dripped from any cut made into my skin was not present.

All I could think of was the blinding white light that surrounded the two of us.

One thing was certain.

Malik wasn't human.

PART 13

Dominic Ronove
Sunday, 5:34pm

Malik had texted several times since he had left.

Thank you, I had an amazing night.

Can we see each other again?

Are you free later?

I responded in kind to each of them. Malik was definitely one human I had intentions on keeping around for a while.

Elisha and Rodolfo didn't count as human anymore. They were marked. They were mine.

I sat at my desk waiting for Elisha to return. I had sent her off on a most important task. She was due back any minute.

Rodolfo was out washing the Benz.

I had the apartment to myself.

Flipping through the spell book I had acquired from the sibling witches, I became increasingly uncomfortable with the level of knowledge, complexity, and power this tome held against my kin. Why on earth would Mammon want to gift this to white witches? What end game was he playing.

But while I was skimming through the massive book, memories of the previous night and Malik's brand kept returning to the forefront of my thoughts. In fact, it became so persistant I abandoned my task and began searching out the unusual sear in the vast collection of archaic texts I had accumulated over the years.

I was looking for something Sumerian? No…it didn't look quite that old.

The flow of the script definitely reminded me of writing I had seen before.

I flipped through some books I had, but nothing came from it.

And then…

A soft knock came from the other side of my office door.

"Yes?" I could scent jasmine. Elisha was back.

"Dominic, are you free?" She asked.

"Yes, please, come in." I closed the book in front of me and tidied up my desk so that anything I had been looking at wasn't front and center. No one needed to know anything about Malik. "Is it done? Did you acquire her?"

"I did. And I had a delightful time doing so. You didn't tell me she'd be so fiesty. But with the wound to the back of her leg still fresh, she couldn't very well run away from me."

"Where is she now?"

"In Rodolfo's room. Cooling down."

"Ah, so you've completed the final step?"

"Yes, she's bleeding out. Rodolfo likes them almost blue."

"I'm well aware. Very good. No trouble from the brothers then?"

"No, but I had to pull out the juju." Elisha was human. A marked human. And she was old. Much older than appearances might suggest. There have to be some perks to being bound into my servitude. Over the years, both Rodolfo and Elisha had acquired some gifts from me, supernatural abilities, charms and amulets, and tokens of my affection. Elisha's bone clip had the unique ability to imbue the wearer with the ability to stun someone for a short period of time. Basically, Elisha could mesmorize anyone leaving them catatonic for a short period.

"It worked on both of them?" I thought the bone clip would only work on a single individual.

"Apparently." She shrugged.

So in the end, the witch siblings had all been taken care of. The brothers were condemned to me, but had six years until I would show up in their lives again. Their sister on the other hand, the one that had been the most powerful out of all of them was now rended powerless from the careful placement of demon hex script.

But seeing as how Rodolfo had been so amazing, saving my ass several times over the course of the last few days, I decided the witch bitch could serve another purpose. Rodolfo did have a prediliction for bodies that were very still and cold.

I nodded to myself and half-grinned. I had chosen my staff well.

I opened a drawer in my desk and pulled out a slim hinged box and handed it to Elisha.

"What's this?"

"Rodolfo got his reward. You get yours. You both do well by me."

Elisha smiled coquetishly, taking the jewelry box, glacing between me and the gift. She carefully opened it.

Her grin grew as she pulled out a necklace that matched her diamond encrusted watch, the one she continued to wear, despite my dislike of its opulence.

"Here, let me." I stood up from my chair, walked around my desk and assisted Elisha in adorning her new trinket. "I should think this would complement the watch nicely."

"You're too good to me." She laid a hand over the diamond studded chain and blushed. She leaned forward and placed a thank you peck on my cheek. "But I have other things to go do, and you need to prepare for tomorrow afternoon. One thirty-five you need to be at the remote office."

"Ah, yes. Very good then. You'll bring the contract so I can review it?"

"Yes. I have to go downstairs to the vault and retrieve it, but I'll be back up shortly." And with that, and a beaming smile, still fondling her necklace, she left.

As the door closed I turned my attention back to the books I had pulled.

Malik's brand.

I flipped back to the section I had been leafing through when some writing caught my attention. It wasn't the same as what I'd seen…but there was a distinct similarity.

A lightbulb. A little flickering flame of recognition.

My eyes went wide.

"It couldn't be."

I ran across the room to another shelf and was just about to pull out the book where I was sure I'd find the answer, when a knock sounded loudly from my front door.

"What the fuck?" Elisha had already gone downstairs, which meant either I answered the door, or let it be.

I ignored the request for entrance.

Pulling the desired book from the shelf – the one I knew where I'd find Malik's mark - the knock came again. This time more insistent and louder.

"For fuck's sake, they're going to break down the goddamn door." Grunting out of displeasure at being disturbed, I placed the book that might contain my answers onto my desk and walked out of my office and toward the front door.

I peered through the peephole.

Then furrowed my brows.

It was Malik's roommate, Scott.

Opening the door, I stood in front of him, crossing my arms, arching an eyebrow, and staring at the man.

He was sweaty, unkempt, and if I didn't know any better, I would have said he was panting. Definitely out of breath. He was also visibly upset.

"Scott, what can I do for you."

He snarled at me, raising a corner of his mouth exposing rather sharp pointed canines. He took a step toward me ignoring society's rules of personal space, and jabbed a finger into my chest. Not jestures that would ensure a welcome response from any of my kind, and seeing as how I didn't like to be touched, the fires of hell were being stoked. Scott was threatening me, and it wouldn't end well for him if he continued.

"Leave. Him. Alone." The words came out more of growl than an actual sentence, each word accompanied by a poke.

I arched an eyebrow. Who the hell did this guy think he was?

"Well, I don't think it's your place to curtail whatever actions Malik wants to take. I assure you he came here last night of his own free will. He also came in bed of his own free will too. Made a glorious mess." I wanted to rile this bastard up, and if this was some display of jealousy,

132

any sordid detail of my tryst with Malik the night before would do exactly that.

"You fucker. He's not yours. He belongs to us. You stay the fuck away from him." Scott snapped at me. Teeth clamping, fangs chomping. His eyes glowed red.

Scott's fist turned into a ball as he reached back and swung toward me. I ducked as his knuckles hit the door frame, splintering the wood.

I registered a small amount of shock. The strength required to do that was well beyond a human's ability.

What the actual fuck?

"You leave your filthy demon claws off of him. He's ours. I won't tell you again."

And with that, Scott turned and stomped off down the hallway, but as he left, he raised one arm, extended his fingers, and tore into the wall.

His nails thick and black, sharp and dangerous penetrated into the plaster leaving a massive claw mark as he dragged his paw all the way down the hall.

Would appear that Scott wasn't as human as he had let on either. More interesting is why I didn't detect him for what he was – a werewolf.

But now that he had exposed himself to me, there would be no second-guessing his nature. Scott's red eyes glared back at me as he glanced over his shoulder, before busting through the stairwell door at the end of the hallway.

The resulting slam reverbated through the floor, and I hoped would not attract the attention of any lower neighbors. This floor was completely owned by me. The last thing I needed though, were for the Chin family beneath me to coming running upstairs.

So, now I had another mystery on my plate.

133

Why was some demon handing over powerful books to witches and trying to get rid of me?

What was Malik?

And why did his roommate – a werewolf – seem to think Malik belonged to him?

This afternoon was getting more and more aggravating as each minute went by.

The damage to the hallway would have to be repaired. I'd get Rodolfo to get the fixes sorted once he returned and had had his playtime. And where the hell was Elisha. She should have been back by now. Was the vault that much of a disorganized mess? I glanced at my watch and noted the time. It was already early evening, and in the beginning of fall in this northern climate, dusk was settling in.

I shook my head, closed my door and returned to my study. I wanted to peruse the book that might tell me what Malik's mark was.

As I entered my office, Sahir sat behind my desk. He motioned to the door making it slam shut.

"Please, have a seat." He gestured toward my oversized Queen Anne chairs positioned near the fireplace. One of them slid over placing itself on the opposite side of my desk.

I glared at him.

Where the fuck did he come from?

The last thing I had right now was patience. And no vampire was going to infiltrate my domain and tell me what I was going to do.

"How the hell did you get in here?" I snapped.

"With me." A voice from the shadows boomed out, and as if appearing out of nothing, Mammon stood in my study. Dressed impeccably in all black, his presence seemed larger than life.

"Mammon. I should've guessed."

134

"What is it that you think you've guessed?" The demon snidely retorted.

"Well, for one, your presence answers how Sahir entered my abode without my invitation. Only you could have brought him here."

A little known fact – Mammon might be one of the Princes of Hell, but he was also my half-brother, and because he was elder, technically owned anything I did. Complicated demonic laws. Any younger sibling must answer to those born before, and supplicate themselves to the elder being. It was one of the reasons I sought out my freedom topside. Luckily, Dad had agreed.

Mammon and I didn't exactly see eye to eye…on anything.

In fact, he had been furious that our Dark Lord and father, had given me free rein topside, but hadn't extended that autonomy to him. It was a bitter point that we fought over whenever we ended up in close proximity. And I went to great lengths to ensure that never happened.

"Considering some recently acquired information," I gestured to the ancient and powerful spell book I had retrieved from the witch siblings' household, "I'm surprised you'd show up here. Daddy won't be too happy with you when he finds out you were giving away family secrets. Thankfully I've managed to secure the book you gave away. Of all the asinine things to do! If I take this little nugget of knowledge to *Dad* I imagine he won't be too happy you gave this much power to a coven of white witches capable of causing our brethren a lot of damage."

"You don't understand anything. You always were completely short-sighted."

"What the fuck am I missing? You've wanted me chained and held prisoner downstairs since I was forged from the brimstone. You've always been jealous of what The King of Hell bestowed on me. What you keep failing to grasp is that I *work* for my rewards where you simply think they should come to you out of some archaic law that states you get it all first. So, kindly fuck off. I have shit to do." Did I ever. I needed to figure out Malik, and deal with Scott. Then I had a contract that was going to come due tomorrow. That required some planning.

"You're such an idiot." Mammon strode forward and much like Scott, got in my space. "The book comes with us, and you are to cease and desist your indulgence with the boy."

"The boy? What boy?"

"The human you bed last night. It was disgusting how you lost control. You don't think that ripple of power you unleashed wasn't felt by everyone else? For fuck's sake Dominic, stick to your lane. You collect souls." He waved his hands through the air while saying it, making light of what I did, dismissing my importance. "I have bigger prey to fetch."

"And Malik is your prey? I don't think so. Now that I know that, I'll be doing everything I can to ensure you get nowhere near him. Count on that."

"You don't have the balls or ability to thwart me."

"You wanna try me?"

Sahir interrupted us.

"Alright boys. Time to put your toys away, as you clearly haven't learned to share." Sahir stood up, smoothed out his clothes, and continued. "Dominic, the boy is special. And he doesn't know it. Yet. He will, soon. When that happens, whoever happens to be on his side stands a chance at gaining some...how shall we say...leverage. And let's face it, we're all striving for additional leverage. Our kind tends to be a little greedy when it comes to the pomp and circumstance around position, nobility, power...those little things.

"You let us take care of him, and we'll make sure you're included on some of the benefits. And if you kindly step to the side, then you can

136

have your puppy back. Does that sound more reasonable?"

"Sahir, what the hell?" Mammon stared at the vampire. The anger and hate were palpable.

"Mammon, if you want to get things done, your way, there have to be some concessions, and sometimes a little bartering. Right? Remember what we talked about?" Sahir prompted Mammon, but an enraged demon is a hard beast to wrangle. "The dog. Bring back the dog and maybe Dominic will play nice."

"Fuck this." Mammon snarled but snapped his fingers. With the *pop* from his motion, a naked, charred, and bloody Cerberus lay at my feet. "There. Don't say I never gave you anything. The boy is ours. Back off, and sit down. Stay where you belong."

Cerberus whined in pain. It was an awful noise.

"You torched my dog?" I glanced at him laying near my feet. I would need both Rodolfo and Elisha to help me get him cleaned up, bandaged, and on the mend. But being a hellhound, he'd survive. He'd have a few more scars to add to the litany of flesh marks he already owned. "And if you think I'm the *only* one who's after Malik, you'd best be talking to his roommate. He showed up before you did. Apparently, he has a claim on him as well. Looks like you have competition from all sides."

"You think a fucking pack of dogs is going to deter me? Those degenerates were once our pets. I'm not letting some feral mutts get any piece of this. Sahir, grab the book. We are out of here. Dominic, remember what I told you. Stay in your damned lane. This doesn't belong to you."

And with that, and a burst of smoke and ash, Mammon and Sahir were gone.

So was the tome I had placed on my desk.

"Dammit"

What the hell was going on?

However, the book I had placed beside the grimoire was still there. I picked it up.

It was the Qur'an. Flipping through its pages and the endless amount of drivel contained within it, I found what I was looking for.

The mark that had been on Malik's back.

It was the symbol for Allah. For God. Also for one specific creature.

The Guardian Angel of Hellfire.

Well, fuck me sideways.

Malik was an angel.